Day of Two Sunsets

Day of Two Sunsets

Paddling Adventures on Canada's West Coast

Michael Blades

ORCA BOOK PUBLISHERS

First edition

Canadian Cataloguing in Publication Data
Blades, Michael, 1944–
    The day of two sunsets

    ISBN 1-55143-001-0
    1. Sea kayaking–British Columbia–Pacific Coast.   2. Pacific Coast
(B.C.)–Description and travel.   3. Sea kayaking–British
Columbia–Vancouver Island.   4. Vancouver Island (B.C.)–Description
and travel.   I. Title.
GV788.5.B53 1993   797.1'224'09711   C93-091638-7

Cover design by Christine Toller
Cover painting and interior illustrations by Jim Ketilson
Back cover photograph by Mike Sheehan

Publication assistance provided by The Canada Council
Printed and bound in Canada

Orca Book Publishers
PO Box 5626, Station B
Victoria, BC   Canada
V8R 6S4

Orca Book Publishers
Box 3028, 1574 Gulf Road
Point Roberts, WA   USA
98281

For Camila,
Jessa and Callum

Although the material for this book has come primarily from my journals, it would not have been completed without the constant support of family, friends, and colleagues at work. For that, I thank you all.

Special acknowledgement for their critical thoughts and timely encouragement go to: Bob Tyrrell, Mike Sheehan, Betty Gilgoff, Wendy Amos, Stephen Bishop, Philip Teece, Robert Gilgoff, and Betty Cavendish.

My sincere appreciation to Jan Blades, Ann Kilbertus, Mike Sheehan, and Chris Blades for their creative assistance, and to Jim Ketilson for his evocative art work.

And not to forget my debt to Gary Nicks, a one-man consumer-reports guru on outdoor equipment.

The journeys in this book would not have been undertaken without the blessings of my wife, Jan, who has always understood my need to go. To her I owe the deepest appreciation.

Whether you travel in your own kayak, or in your imagination, it is my hope that these simple stories will lift you up and carry you along, and that in the end we will all come to a deeper appreciation of uncluttered places.

CONTENTS

The most beautiful thing we can experience
is the mysterious

— Albert Einstein

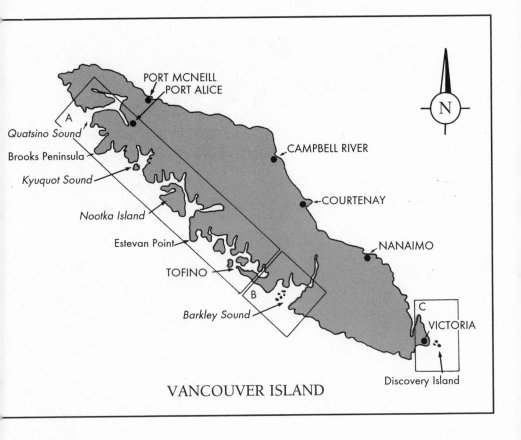

PORT MCNEILL
PORT ALICE

A

Quatsino Sound

Brooks Peninsula

Kyuquot Sound

Nootka Island

Estevan Point

TOFINO

B

Barkley Sound

CAMPBELL RIVER

COURTENAY

NANAIMO

C

VICTORIA

Discovery Island

VANCOUVER ISLAND

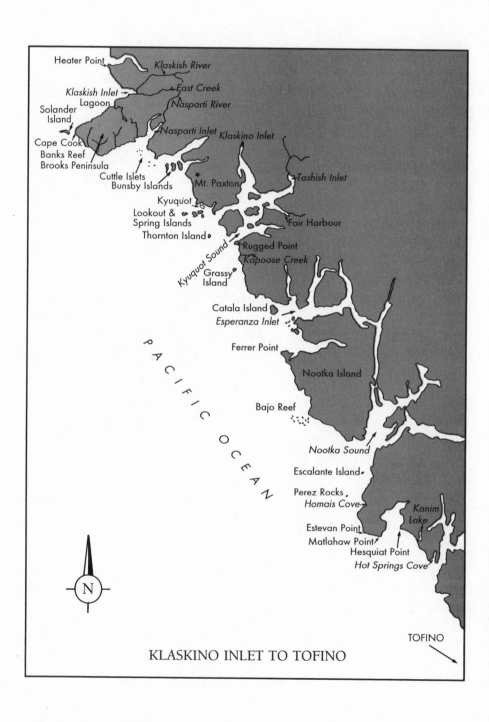

Heater Point
Klaskish River
Klaskish Inlet
East Creek
Lagoon
Nasparti River
Solander
Island
Nasparti Inlet Klaskino Inlet
Cape Cook
Banks Reef
Brooks Peninsula
Cuttle Islets
Bunsby Islands
Mt. Paxton
Tashish Inlet
Kyuquot
Lookout &
Spring Islands
Fair Harbour
Thornton Island
Rugged Point
Kapoose Creek
Kyuquot Sound
Grassy
Island
Catala Island
Esperanza Inlet
Ferrer Point
Nootka Island
Bajo Reef
Nootka Sound
Escalante Island
Perez Rocks
Homais Cove
Kanim Lake
Estevan Point
Matlahaw Point
Hesquiat Point
Hot Springs Cove

P A C I F I C   O C E A N

N

TOFINO

KLASKINO INLET TO TOFINO

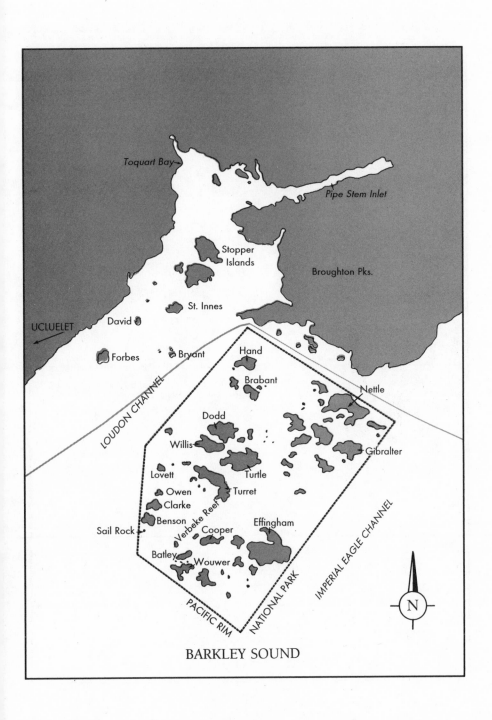

BARKLEY SOUND

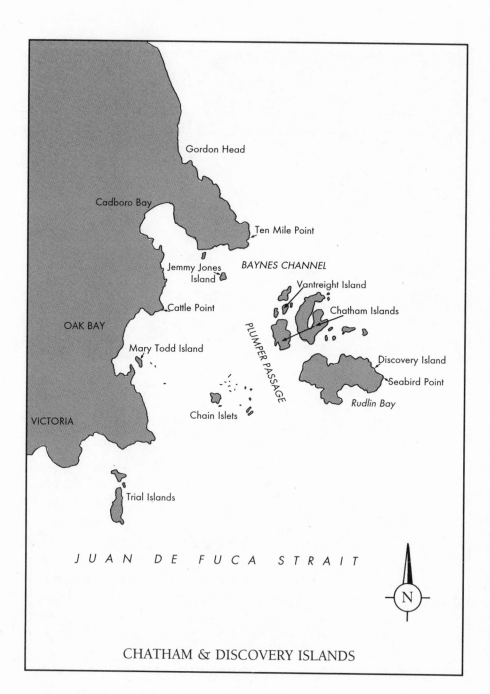

Gordon Head

Cadboro Bay

Ten Mile Point

Jemmy Jones Island

BAYNES CHANNEL

Vantreight Island

Chatham Islands

Cattle Point

OAK BAY

Mary Todd Island

PLUMPER PASSAGE

Discovery Island

Seabird Point

Rudlin Bay

Chain Islets

VICTORIA

Trial Islands

J U A N   D E   F U C A   S T R A I T

N

CHATHAM & DISCOVERY ISLANDS

INTRODUCTION

I LOOKED AGAIN back over my right shoulder. A dark
green ocean swell, the size of a house, roared down upon
me. Sitting in my sixteen-foot kayak, I felt like a little child
in a toy boat about to be obliterated. Flecks of white built on
the approaching crest and formed into a wave upon a wave.
The top three feet curled, then exploded down upon itself.
Seconds later the massive wall of water swept under me and I
shot upward at a frightening speed. As the sea of white foam
engulfed the kayak, I quickly braced on my outstretched paddle to prevent a capsize. For a moment I sat high above the
world and searched for any sign of my paddling companion,
Mike. At first I saw nothing, then suddenly he and his kayak
appeared, looking small and insignificant in the rough seas.
The look on his face was intense. Then he was gone and I
dropped into what seemed a bottomless trough between the

giant walls of water. To my rear, the next mountain of dark green moved swiftly towards me.

We were rounding Cape Cook, also known as the Cape of Storms, off the northwest coast of Vancouver Island. The wind and sea conditions were very close to the limit that I ever wanted to experience; I could feel fear bubbling in healthy proportions inside me. A few minutes later I passed alongside Mike and shouted above the howling wind, "If we get out of here in one piece will you remind me why it is we *choose* to do this!" He turned, flashed a wide grin, then was erased from view as the next swell rose up between us.

A little more than an hour later we stood on a beautiful pebble and sand beach nestled in a well-protected cove. Forty- to fifty-knot winds roared over the mountains behind us, shooting well out to sea. Where we stood, however, all was calm. It was wonderful to be safe, dry, and basking in the warm sun. I lay back on the beach and the heat from the pebbles crept into my tired body. My muscles turned off the "full alert" switch and started to ooze into a soft, relaxed state. An eagle, perched high on a towering Sitka spruce, cried out. Behind us, the tops of the tallest trees bent seaward, while their massive trunks provided us with a wall of peaceful protection from the strong winds. I closed my eyes.

Later, I sat up and sipped some of the cool clear water we'd collected from a steep mountain stream on the north side of the Brooks Peninsula. I shifted and leaned back against a warm rock; a hint of movement caught my eye. From under a grey log a little mouse appeared. It paused, looked about, then scurried across a stretch of white sand, through the hollow formed by a fresh bear track, and disappeared into a tiny crevice in a giant rock.

Having survived the sudden and unexpected storm to kiss these blessed shores, I could now put the whole experience into the "I'm glad I did it but do not plan to ever repeat it" category. Pondering the question I'd flung out to Mike: "Why do we *choose* to do this?" was a luxury which could now be indulged.

My increasing obsession with ocean kayaking had not been with the purpose of embarking upon high-risk, death-defying journeys. Initially, the kayak had simply been a means to get away from the confines and clatter of civilization. Then I discovered the magic of travelling the special corridor between open ocean and rugged shoreline. The kayak was the perfect craft. It was designed to sneak through narrow channels on rock-strewn coasts and to slide onto beaches where few others had been. The limits of my own physical strength and skills, coupled with the need for an acute awareness of my surroundings, acted as a simple but powerful motivation to be in the "now." Failure to see the reef that lay ahead, or the increase in a changing current, could easily spell serious trouble. The water, sky, and land all became an open book, full of wonder and information. Unfortunately, they were written in a language I was only slowly coming to learn. Still, each journey provided an ever deeper understanding, as well as an increased sense of kinship with the earth.

In my work at the hospital, as a pediatric social worker, I was often involved with families whose children had died. The impact of these deaths carried over into my personal life. The children, and their parents, taught me valuable lessons. I learned that although it was important to have dreams and goals, it was equally necessary to count my blessings and to value each day as a gift. The message was similar to what I'd heard from many old folk, who with the hindsight of a lifetime, talked of worrying less, smelling the flowers more, and appreciating the wonder and mystery of daily life.

It all seemed to point strongly to the notion that satisfaction and contentment did not exist in some other time or place, but rather right here, where I sat today. A sign on my wall at work summed it up:

Rush Slowly.
Keep Breathing.
This Is It.

The challenge, of course, is to lift this wisdom off the wall and make it come alive. Slowing down seemed a wonderful first step, and the kayak could not have provided a better means for doing so.

BEGINNINGS

BEGINNINGS

TO THIS DAY I'm not really sure what drew me into ocean kayaking. A part of me wonders if there wasn't an obtuse connection with an old 650-cc British Motorcycle I'd once owned. To me it had oozed romance, sitting in the fading sun with its deep burgundy coloured tank and my worn homemade saddlebags draped over the rear. I can still vividly recall the wondrous journeys on winding country roads, the joy of smelling spring's perfume in the air, and feeling the subtle temperature shift as I dropped into a valley or hit a shady stretch of road.

Mind you, there were drawbacks. The bike broke down with great regularity, and parts and my mechanical ingenuity were limited. The Lucas electrical system was affectionately known as the "Prince of Darkness" for its unfailing habit of packing it in one hour after sunset, and the engine vibration was constant and numbing. In addition, there was always the pool of oil under the beast — "the mark of Royalty" an old British gent had once tried to assure me.

Eventually I sold the motorcycle, but I still have warm memories, not only for all the journeys made, but also for everything the bike represented. There was simplicity, a freedom, and always a sense of adventure.

And so it was that when I passed the sign in the store window advertising "An Introduction to Ocean Kayaking," I walked in and signed up. Perhaps just on a whim, but maybe still seeking some of that freedom, simplicity, and adventure from the old motorcycle days. The cost of the course was only fifty dollars and the time required was a Friday night and a weekend. I knew nothing about ocean kayaking, and although I'd spent a lot of time on the water, it had always been with a screaming outboard. The subtleties of wind and current knowledge were unknown to me. If the current was against me I simply cranked up the throttle.

The evening lecture introduced information on kayak shapes, materials, and safety. There was talk on wind, currents, clothing, and equipment. On Saturday we all practised capsizing in the University pool and making good our escape. We also slapped our paddles vigorously on the water, attempting to mimic the high and low braces of our instructors — techniques whereby one tilted the kayak on its edge with knee and thigh movements, while momentarily leaning for support on the flat side of an outstretched paddle (a quick snap of the hips theoretically flicked one upright to the vertical). On the Sunday, about twelve of us climbed into an assortment of single and double kayaks for our first experience on the ocean. It was a warm, early day in spring, with little wind. We paddled out of Oak Bay, through the Chain Islets, to Discovery Island.

I remember nothing profound about the day. No flash of intuitive oneness with nature. No voice spoke to my inner core. In fact, the return trip almost put me off the whole idea of kayaking. I'd elected to try a double kayak, and about one hundred yards into the return trip my partner's wrist gave out and I had the thrill of paddling the heavy slug of a craft back single-handed. Yet somehow, somewhere, there was a part of me that must have known the possibilities.

Over the summer a couple of friends and I rented some kayaks. With good fortune and fine weather we enjoyed some delightful sunny day paddles. Then, in August, we took the plunge and prepared for our first weekend trip. We rented three kayaks and drove out to the village of Sidney. When we arrived, the tide was already well out. I drove my old van onto the sloping beach and we began the process of unloading the kayaks, adjusting rudder pedals, sorting spray skirts, and squeezing what seemed to be an infinite amount of gear into the three slim craft.

It took us almost an hour. By then the tide had turned and the kayaks floated quietly, their sleek lines begging to cut through the morning calm. It was a warm, sunny day; a soft breeze barely rippled the water. We eased out and with only moderate anxiety charted a course over to Forrest Island. A few "tupperware" powerboats roared by, shattering the silence and breaking the ocean's smoothness with their bulky forms. In contrast, our own craft moved easily on the surface, barely disturbing the water. Only the tiny whirl-pools left by the paddles told of our passing.

And oh but it was such a peaceful way to travel. The world was alive, not so much with noise as with sound. The gulls whirled and cried with delight as they circled a ball of feed, and a sea lion broke the surface with a tremen-dous "whoosh," then plunged downward. Waves lapped on the shore of a nearby islet and oystercatchers cried out when we passed too close. A heron, upset by our presence, startled us with its loud prehistoric squawk. It slowly lifted its delicate frame into the air, then glided away on out-stretched wings.

Eventually our slow, rhythmic paddling brought us to Forrest Island. We found a delightful cove, with pebble and sand beach, almost completely enclosed by rock. Seeing no signs of occupancy, we decided to camp at the shore's edge.

An old shack stood nearby, leaning precariously to one side. It had obviously been here some time, for it blended in with the tall grass and trees, with a sense of its own place.

We set up camp and then returned to the kayaks, paddling slowly through the kelp and shallow waters over an off-shore reef. A baby seal, soft silver in colour, nestled on a rock with its mother. Despite our quiet, slow approach, drifting only on the current, we were soon perceived. Mom, with a healthy sense of wariness, flopped awkwardly down the rock and slithered into the cool depths where she was in her element. The babe followed quickly. With awe we sat and watched the two swim in the crystal-clear waters under our craft. At one point the mother's puppy dog face quietly rose near my boat. She eyed me gently, then nostrils closed, and with the smoothness of melting ice cream, she slipped under and disappeared.

By September, my seduction was almost complete. I now fully subscribed to a friend's opinion that the downfall of mankind had begun with the invention of the internal combustion engine. Ironically, it was only a short while ago that I was the one hurtling along in a fourteen-foot runabout, leaving a cloud of noxious blue vapour behind. When I'd spied people in kayaks, rowboats, or simple sailing craft, I'd been unable to comprehend their apparent stupidity. The motor obviously got you there faster and with less effort. Now I was rapidly becoming one of those fanatical born again souls . . . the kayak was the *only* way to go.

One evening in early fall, while walking along the shore with my wife, I spied a very tall, bearded man preparing to launch his kayak. I shyly ventured over to talk. His name was Mike Sheehan and he'd been paddling for years, much of it solo, up in the Queen Charlottes and out on the exposed west coast of Vancouver Island. He was kind, tolerant of my ignorance, and very supportive of my enthusiasm. Later I stood on the shore and watched him paddle out in the soft evening light. I slipped over the edge, past the point of no return, and that week bought my first kayak.

It was a used craft, well maintained. Its soft grey colour was polished to a high sheen with repeated coats of aircraft wax on its fibreglass shell. Its previous owner had obviously loved and cared for it well. Alas, he and his wife had become separated while paddling their singles in stormy weather. Upon landing safely on shore she had announced, in a voice which left no room for mediation, that if he wished her company on future trips they would be paddling in a double. And thus he sadly traded in the grey beauty. His misfortune became my blessing.

Several nights later I again walked the shore. This time, however, the evening was quite different. The sky was overcast, and dark, menacing clouds moved quickly along the horizon. A strong wind whipped the waves into sharp seas. They were grey and ugly. This was *not* the sort of weather in my romantic kayaking fantasies. It looked cold, frightening, and dangerous. I faltered. Doubt crept in. Why had I just bought this damn thing? It was all based on idyllic dreams and a few sun-drenched days of kayaking. Fool!

It was then that I noticed Mike's car at the roadside, ropes hanging down from the roof rack. "My God," I thought. "He's out there paddling. He must know what he's doing . . . or else he's crazy." (Later I was to decide there was truth in both statements.) I scribbled a note and stuck it under his windshield wiper: "Don't know if you remember me. Stopped to talk with you the other evening. Have purchased a kayak but could sure do with some skilled company on my initial paddles in less than ideal conditions. If you think you might be able to join me sometime, would much appreciate a call . . . "

Mike called that evening, and we arranged a paddle for the upcoming weekend. It was to be the first of many, venturing out to Discovery, Chatham, and Darcy islands on blustery fall and winter days. Later I accompanied Mike out to the west coast of Vancouver Island, embarking upon extended journeys where we'd see no other human for weeks, and the only prints we'd find on shore belonged to wolf or bear.

It was to become all I dreamed, and more.

KAPOOSE

KAPOOSE

~~~~~

IT WAS AN eight-hour drive from Victoria to Fair Harbour on Vancouver Island's northwest coast. The last stretch had been over rough logging road and it was with relief that I finally stepped out of the truck. I was excited, nervous, and generally uncomprehending of what lay ahead. I'd taken up ocean kayaking about a year and a half ago under the guidance of my friend Mike, and had begun testing the waters off Victoria on a regular basis. According to my wife, my love for kayaking had now gone beyond anything resembling a healthy interest.

Already I was on to my second kayak. It was a smaller, more responsive craft, in which I felt most comfortable, even in rough seas. The drawback was its reduction in cargo space. Fortunately, I usually paddled with Mike and thus my problem was solved. Being 6'5", he owned a large boat. All excess gear was thus easily stashed in his craft. Our trips together resulted in his kayak often weighing a good third more than mine. I thought this wonderful, as it provided me with the chance to keep up with his powerful and quick paddling.

A few weeks earlier Mike had asked if I wanted to accompany him on a paddle off the northwest coast of Vancouver Island. I eagerly accepted. He assured me that the outer coast experience would be something quite different from anything I'd done to date, and something I'd not forget. I didn't understand what he was talking about. Despite living most of my life in British Columbia, I was lost when he talked of Kyuquot, the Bunsbys, and the Brooks Peninsula. I had to dig out a chart and have these places shown to me. Now, here I was, at the head of Kyuquot Sound, 4:00 PM, on a warm August day. Although tired from the drive, we decided it would be nice to head out immediately and get away from the other vehicles and campers.

While in the process of accomplishing the impossible — getting what appeared to be a mountain of *basic* supplies into such tiny boats — a woman walked over from a nearby vehicle. She and Mike discussed paddling itineraries, then after wishing us a safe journey, she returned to her companion, who was preparing to load their kayaks.

"You know her?" I asked.

"I've met her before," replied Mike. "Her name's Ros."

"That's sure a narrow kayak she's got," I said. "She must be pretty good."

"You might say that," laughed Mike. "She's the one who paddled eleven hundred miles through the Northwest Passage with a friend."

Talk about putting things in perspective. Here I was getting somewhat anxious about the fifteen miles that lay ahead!

Eventually we finished loading and launched into a moderate wind. For whatever reason, Mike decided not to take the northern arm of Kyuquot Sound, which would have been the most direct route to the Bunsbys. Instead, we travelled the southern course, a choice that turned out to be ideal. Mike learned later that Ros and her friend encountered over thirty-eight paddlers on their trip! We were to see only two.

That night we made camp on a tiny beach, still deep in the Sound. It was idyllic, except for the mosquitoes and no-see-ums, which eventually drove me into the sanctity of my tent to finish dinner. It was the first and only time that bugs would be a problem. After dinner I sat and watched the setting sun. Seals surfaced and salmon leapt, creating distant rippling pools. It was very quiet. Each sound stood alone and distinct.

Early next morning we packed and launched into a gem of a day. The sky was cloudless, the sea calm, with only a hint of breeze. We set course for Rugged Point at the mouth of Kyuquot Sound. Salmon broke the surface all around us. A friendly heron flew low overhead and landed on a nearby rock. The ebb pushed us along nicely, and what little wind there was came at our backs. And then, even on this calmest of days, I felt the open ocean. Today it was a gentle, never ending, rolling, rolling, incoming swell after swell. I could not have asked for a kinder introduction to something so powerful.

We pulled into the protected cove behind Rugged Point and followed the trail that wove amongst the towering trees, stuffing our faces with succulent huckleberries. The beach we came upon was out of a dream. Pure soft sand, gentle unfolding surf, brilliant blue sky, and no one else. Mike stood at the shore's edge, scanning the ocean with his binoculars. "Over there!" he shouted. I looked, saw only open expanse, distant rocky islets, and a small, faint cloud of mist. Then he shouted again, and pointed. My first grey whale broke the surface. The telltale spume of mist rose gently in the air, then it was gone.

Although Mike had been out this way before, he'd always explored northward. This time he suggested we go south and see what the possibilities might be of landing at a small creek marked on the chart as "Kapoose."

"I haven't seen it this calm before," he said. "Let's go!"

We paddled out on the softly rising swell and through

the mildly confused seas off Rugged Point. The haunting moan of the channel marker came from further out. We turned and headed south. Suddenly the whale rose, only thirty yards off my bow. What a moment!

We made our way on through rock, reef, and around seastacks. I followed Mike with a blind faith. He seemed to perceive an ocean pathway, invisible to my eye, that bent and twisted through all the danger. At this stage I had little awareness of the skill, judgement, and inner sense required to *see* these paths. My mind was elsewhere, struck by the power of even this mild sea, which thundered in upon exposed rock and hidden reef. I was quite overwhelmed by the wild beauty of it all.

Looking at the surf rolling in on a series of long curving beaches, I wondered how we would manage to land undamaged. Then, at the extreme end of the white sand, we slid past a rocky outcrop, avoided the breaking surf, and drifted into the clear, light-green waters at the mouth of Kapoose Creek. The tide was flooding and we were able to paddle up the creek right to the forest's edge. We stepped out on the immaculate beach. It was all ours.

We set up camp above the high tide line, under the shelter of a towering spruce. Kapoose Creek wound past our doorstep. Twenty yards away in the damp sand we discovered fresh wolf tracks.

In the evening, as the sun slowly set, Mike insisted we stare intently and look for the elusive green flash that can sometimes be glimpsed on the horizon at the moment of last light. Alas, even with the aid of some Cointreau, it escaped us. Later, the near-to-full moon rose, turning the beach a soft magical white. The busy world of work and city seemed far, far away.

In the days that followed we made numerous paddles out to nearby islands and islets. I learned why August was called "Fogust," and that by noon on a hot day the calm morning winds could easily rise to twenty-five knots or more. Several grey whales appeared resident in our area, and often they would surface nearby. It never ceased to amaze me how gentle they seemed. It never dawned on me to feel nervous.

My feelings about the ocean, however, became a different matter. As my eyes began to open, a healthy respect and level of fear began to rapidly develop. One day, coming back from exploring Grassy Island, we found ourselves in most uncomfortable conditions. A distant fog bank moved quickly towards us. The following ocean swell had increased dramatically in size, and Mike, paddling ahead of me, often disappeared completely from view. Problems compounded when large breaking waves appeared directly on the port beam. The seas became rough and confused, and for the first time I had to attempt bracing. I awkwardly tried to imitate what they'd shown us in the University pool, in what seemed a very long-ago kayak course. My style was pathetic, but the general gist was okay, and I managed to stay right side up. Instead of things becoming a disaster or a terror-ridden ride, it became an exhilarating and healthy step in gaining essential experience. I was thankful it was warm and sunny. It would have been a nightmare had all been cold, grey, and covered in fog.

Several days later we paddled out to the Volcanic Islets. They were covered with seabirds, and we quietly drifted alongside the rugged cliffs. Later, I pulled out my little collapsible fishing rod and after only one cast hooked a nice-sized lingcod for dinner. On our return, Mike continued on to the campsite, while I pulled into an adjacent beach to clean the fish. No need to attract bears to our doorstep.

I had developed a healthy paranoia about bears in the last few days. I'd gone for a walk by myself through the giant Sitka spruce on the other side of Kapoose Creek. Brilliant shafts of sunlight had filtered through the forest canopy. I felt a deep sense of peace . . . until I turned a corner and found a humungous pile of steaming-hot bear faeces. It was rather a profound moment, realizing I was not alone in the Garden of Eden. Since then, we had noted an abundance of bear sign and had taken extra precautions not to attract big, furry visitors.

I cleaned the ling quickly and easily, storing it in a zip-lock bag, with a touch of seawater. Paddling back to camp, I could see no sign of Mike or his kayak. Then I noticed him well down the beach, paddling broadside to the incoming surf, practising high and low braces. It seemed that, after our experience the other day, he had decided this was a good opportunity to brush up on some rather rusty skills.

The surf was mild to moderate, and both wind and tide were incoming. The sun beat down on an incredibly hot day. It was ideal. I paddled nervously along, parallel to the waves. I soon found it easy to tilt the craft with thigh and knee pressure into the breaking swells, extending the paddle in the same direction, flat side of the blade on the water. In this manner I could literally be supported while being swept into shore. My cockiness increased when I looked up and saw Mike standing in waist-deep water, his kayak upside down a short distance away. "Hah, hah, even the master can capsize!" I chuckled to myself.

I paddled out through the waves, then turned and had a real thrill surfing in on the swell. On the next run I suddenly found myself hurtling down the front of a particularly steep wave, in very shallow water. My speed increased. Instead of leaning back or bracing, I fell forward. The bow plunged to the bottom and dug into the sand. The swell rose up, lifting my stern almost to the vertical. Mike looked on in horror as I wailed, "Oh no!"

It was then that my guardian angel decided the time had not yet arrived for me to become a paraplegic. The wave did not break and flip me in cartwheel fashion. Instead, it rode under the kayak, lifting the bow from its sandy grip, allowing the stern to quickly drop to the surface. Terror and embarrassment swept through me in equal measure.

I abandoned surfing and timidly returned to practising high and low braces. A larger-than-normal wave suddenly rose above me. I half-heartedly braced. WHAM! I was whirled about as though in a washing machine, then literally blown out of my kayak. Eventually I found myself standing intact in chest-deep water; my capsized kayak lay to my left, my paddle to the right, and all the loose junk I carried in the cockpit, from rope to fish fillets, floated on the surface.

Humbling to say the least.

It was a day of unforgettable lessons. My respect for the sea grew immeasurably. Gear was no longer stacked loosely in the cockpit; everything soon found a proper place, firmly attached. We continued to practise over the next few days, and it was one of the most valuable confidence- and skill-building exercises I could ever have dreamed up.

And so the time passed.

Eventually the day came when we found ourselves enjoying the last evening meal. Our VHF radio advised of an impending decline in the weather, which made the thought of departing much easier. We rose at 2:00 AM with high hopes of paddling out under the full moon. Unfortunately, the approaching low had already brought in a thick layer of cloud; all light was extinguished. We rose again at 4:00, but it was equally dark. At 6:00 AM we broke camp and slipped out through the mouth of Kapoose Creek.

"And as they came, so they went," I heard Mike say.

Not a whiff of wind stirred the air; the sea was flat. Early light reflected on the water's gentle, undulating surface, and large, dark clouds loomed on the distant horizon.

Rounding Rugged Point the wind freshened at our backs, in delightful contrast to the expected headwind. It was an easy paddle the remaining distance to Fair Harbour.

The gods had smiled most favourably on this inaugural journey of mine. I knew I would be back.

THORNTON

THORNTON

~~~~~

THE FOLLOWING YEAR, in mid-June, we returned to Kapoose Creek.

It was a hard first day's paddle. The wind blew constantly, head on, the entire distance to Rugged Point. Waves often rode over the deck, making for damp, chilling conditions. Our kayaks also seemed exceedingly heavy. Somehow the list of "basic" supplies had expanded, and supreme skill was required to get it all aboard. In the end there was no room for the four-litre wine sack, so it had to be lashed on my rear deck. (I was sure that the bottles from which I'd poured the wine had clearly stated: "Serve chilled." Would exposure to the day's sun cause harm? Ah! Such are the dilemmas of life.)

Of more serious concern in the choppy sea was the fact that water was somehow seeping into my cockpit. After three and a half hours of paddling there was a good couple of inches sloshing around, soaking my bottom and making its way into my boots. Eventually we reached the protected cove behind Rugged Point and pulled in. I spread my wet gear on the warm rocks, sponged the water out of my kayak, and set about finding the source of leakage. I was glad to see that the bulkheads had done their job and everything was dry in the fore and aft holds. Mike opened the crackers, peanut butter, and jam in preparation for lunch. The last of the clouds dissolved in the sky and a hot sun beat down.

After eating, I duct-taped what appeared to be two leak possibilities around the rudder cable openings in the hull. We pushed off and headed out into the Sound. The swells were large, resulting in chaotic conditions off Rugged Point. My kayak handled well and the duct tape seemed to do the trick. Once around the headland, the following seas became moderate and regular. Familiar landmarks stood out and we paddled a safe course through the rock-strewn waters. At the end of a long reef, upon which the incoming swell exploded, we made a hard left into the shallow waters of Kapoose Creek.

The tide was low, but we still managed to manoeuvre in far enough to run the kayaks up onto the sand. We stepped out. The long expanse of beach, bordered by dense forest, was as wild and untouched as I remembered. Our campsite of last year had been erased by winter storms, and I had just set about looking for a new spot when Mike called out. I turned and wandered over to where he was standing, just below the high tide line. He pointed down to three sets of fresh wolf tracks — large, medium, and small. A family? I'd never seen a wolf in the wild, and finding the tracks was almost as good; my imagination conjured up all sorts of visions. We followed the trail and saw where the wolves had stopped and frolicked, then turned and headed up into the trees. We walked back towards the kayaks, then halted. Two eagles, one mature, the other young, flew out of the forest, following the creek's winding course to the ocean. Suddenly they rose steeply, braked and gently settled on separate limbs of a large Sitka spruce. It was easy to start believing in good omens.

We set up camp by the creek under the shade of over-hanging branches, while the eagles looked on. I moved the wine sack into the cool of the shadows. Mike scoured the beach, and, as usual, returned with exactly the right pieces of wood with which we could create a good kitchen.

In honour of the first day's paddle we decided "Kapoose Creek Sandwiches," topped off with a glass of *chilled* white wine, would be in order. Mike set up his stove and cooking gear while I got to buttering one side of each of eight slices of our Wheatberry bread. This done, the Edam cheese was cut in thin strips and the jar of hot sauce opened. Fresh tomatoes were then cut, also in thin layers; a few were quartered, coated with spices, and eaten as an apéritif. I poured the wine.

Cheese and tomato slices were then stacked on the non-buttered side of the bread, sprinkled with an assortment of condiments, and then liberally covered in Mexican hot sauce. The other piece of bread was added and the whole works placed in the now well-heated frying pan. When cooked, the full-bodied bread was warm, with a delightfully crunchy texture. The combination of melted cheese and tomatoes, set off by the sauce and spices, capped a gem of a day. We sipped the cool wine, our backs against a log, and watched the sun prepare to slip into the layer of cloud hovering over the distant Brooks Peninsula.

In the morning we wandered the short distance into the forest where we'd hung the food. We lowered the bag and dug out the goodies necessary for a breakfast of blueberry pancakes. As Mike pulled the bag up, he noticed a pile of old animal droppings. Once the rope was secured, he knelt and examined the scat closely. Breaking it apart, he discovered a bear claw. He brushed it off and gently turned it in his palm, then rose, smiled, and tucked it in his pocket.

We went back to camp and piled the breakfast ingredients and cookware on the small table. We then each took an end, walked out of the shade, and moved the kitchen down to the rocks, which by now were covered with the early morning sun. It was a beautiful day, with the only visible clouds being those still over the Brooks.

The next few days saw us paddling out to Grassy and Clark islands, as well as exploring the coastline well southwards. In the late afternoon we would often return and practise our bracing and paddling in the surf off Kapoose.

One evening, after a particularly fine dinner of fresh fish, we turned on the weather radio. The forecast indicated an approaching low with possible rain. We put up tarps over the tents and kitchen before crawling into bed.

When we rose, it was cloudy but calm. While eating breakfast Mike extolled the charms of Thornton Island, some five to six miles away. The day looked okay, but I felt some apprehension when I examined the chart. There were a lot of rocks, reef, and islets between us and Thornton if we paddled anything resembling a direct course. Still, why not. I agreed to go.

Shortly after starting, the skies cleared and for the next six hours or so it was a hot, sunny day. The sea, however, did not stay flat. There was little wind, but before we'd gone a couple of miles we were encountering very large swells. Mike estimated them to be fifteen to twenty feet high. They were not sharp nor breaking. They would, however, bear down on us at a terribly fast pace, the height of a two-storey house, then miraculously we'd rise up, up, and onto a surface almost as flat as a playing field. Then, it would be down, down into the trough, with all horizon blotted out.

We stayed well off the Rugged Point headland, yet still felt the chaos of swells clashing with the strong ebb. The seas became very confused. As we were headed offshore, I soon lost regular sight of land; my field of vision became filled with seas going left, right, up, down, and every which way. It required steady, nonstop paddling, and on occasion, a quick turn into a huge, swift-moving swell that threatened to break and slam me broadside. Then a new concern emerged. I was beginning to feel seasick. Perhaps the pancakes hadn't been cooked well enough? Argh! How much further?

Mike, on the other hand, appeared to be having a grand time. When I shouted out about my queasiness, he told me it was all in my head! We paddled on, then slowed and paused, well outside the final extensive rock and reef garden between us and Thornton. With the large, powerful swells sweeping in, the whole area resembled an exploding minefield. By myself, I would have taken a much longer route around the whole mess. (Let's be honest ... I wouldn't be here by myself!) Mike, however, stared intently, studying the scene in detail. Then he nodded and shouted, "Let's go!" He dug his paddle deeply into the water and with consummate skill threaded a safe course through to Thornton's protected shore. I followed very closely, as an iron filing to a magnet. With joy in my heart and breakfast nearly in my mouth, I stepped out onto dry land.

The queasiness soon subsided and we set to exploring this magical little place. The island was a series of stony outcroppings with a multitude of red-beaked oystercatchers flitting and crying out amongst the rocks. A sand-shell causeway joined our tiny beach to a small, steep-sided island that was well treed and abundant in beautiful wildflowers. Mike found a vertical ridge that served as the trail upward. A massive old rope, bleached white by the weather, lay beside us as a potential handrail. The rock and cliff were blanketed with the most vivid little flowers — shades of blue, bright yellow, deep blush, and soft white.

At the top of the climb a miniature naked goddess, about a foot high, complete with eyes, breasts, arms, and feet, stood in the tall grass. She'd been made from wooden fishing floats, shells and twigs. She seemed rather tiny to be here all alone, yet she had a regal bearing and her presence seemed welcoming and protective. We climbed a few more steep steps and a lovely little shack, covered in hand-split cedar shakes, came into view. What a setting! A sign over the door announced:

Whaletown Museum
Research Station
"Windy — Villa"
in progress
Welcome

On a day like today, it was a little paradise with magnificent views. On stormy days, I wondered how protected
things would be, perched so high on this rocky island. It
was then that I noticed that the whole structure was
wrapped and firmly tied to the ground with steel cable! I
opened the door and looked inside. It seemed well cared
for. There was a wood stove, a bunk with foam, and some
food staples. (Years later, while on Cortez Island, I was to
meet Pierre and Wendy, who had helped their friend
George build this little hideaway.)

Back outside, we took a narrow path that led upward
through the dense growth. On the way we spied two large
nests, firmly built into trees whose bases lay in a valley
well below us. Upon reaching the top we entered a small
meadow, covered in wild strawberries. Only a short distance away, at eye-level, perched two mature eagles.

We sat quietly. To the north and south we had stupen-
dous views, and for the first time I was able to get an
inkling of the incredible amount of clearcut logging in the
area. Whole mountainsides had been cut from the ocean's
edge, up the steep slopes, right to the peaks. Through my
binoculars I could see that even "forest fringes" left along
shore and creekside had been blown down. It was a most
sobering sight.

The sun was warm and soothing; the meadow lay well
protected from the wind. Then Mike thought he saw the
head of a "wee" one in the nest. We moved away so as not
to disturb the eagles any further and headed back down to
the beach and our kayaks. After lunch we launched and
headed out, back through the explosive, foam-filled minefield, and aimed for the Volcanic Islets off Kapoose.

The swells were as big, if not bigger, than on our out-
ward journey, and now they came from our right rear
quarter. The trick, I quickly learned, was not to get going too
fast. I could feel the rear of my craft suddenly rise under an
approaching swell, and the tendency was to either hurtle
down the face, with the high probability of the bow going
under and one and all becoming a submarine, or of having

the stern pushed sideways, with the likelihood of broaching. I watched Mike carefully, saw how he would pause at
the right moment, maybe even back-paddle a stroke or two,
do a corrective brace, then paddle on. I soon got the idea,
but still found it quite unsettling to look over my shoulder
and see a wall of water the size of a house roaring down
upon me. It seemed a miracle each time the kayak rose up,
instead of being overrun and demolished.

We soon reached the Volcanic Islets and stopped in
their lee. It was so delightfully calm that I took out my
fishing rod and made one quick cast. I was immediately
rewarded with a nice-sized sea trout, more than ample for
dinner. We paddled the remaining one and a half miles
with ease and landed safely on the sandy beach at camp. I
looked back at Thornton through my binoculars. The wind
was now picking up and I could see breaking crests on
some of the large swells. The island seemed so alone, way
out there in this powerful sea. The fragile beauty of its
wildflowers and little meadow made Thornton seem all the
more magical.

The whole experience had also been quite humbling.
The conditions had been the most demanding in which I'd
ever paddled, and the initial stages of seasickness made for
a healthy sense of vulnerability. I also looked at Mike with
increased admiration. He'd come out here on many previous trips by himself, without the aid of a more
knowledgeable soul to guide him along. For me, that in
itself would be a huge challenge. Alone, and with potential
danger, my imagination can run wild. He'd had to find
things out by himself and face his own fears. In addition, I
was only beginning to discover the degree of understanding, experience, and intuition that was required to read the
sea conditions with any reliability. Sitting only a few inches
above the water does not give the nice overview found in
an aerial photograph, and charting a course through rough
and rock-strewn seas is a real art. What further impressed
me was that he was not foolish in his decisions nor prone
to taking high risks. True, just being out here involved risk,

but I'm sure that statistically I ran more chance of injury or death on my daily drive to work. The choices Mike made were well thought out and calculated, and if something didn't seem right, he had no hesitation in changing plans. Still, it was nice to be on shore. The weather certainly seemed to be intensifying.

"I wouldn't be surprised if all this is a precursor to that low they mentioned yesterday," said Mike. "Let's see what goodies Environment Canada has for us."

The voice on the VHF radio gave an updated warning of a fast-approaching, intense low, with gale to storm-force southeasterlies. Our camp was in a relatively protected spot as far as the winds were concerned, so we stayed put and cooked up another superb evening meal with the fish I'd caught earlier. We checked the rain tarps and talked of leaving in the morning if conditions permitted, or perhaps hanging on with the hope that the low would sweep through as quickly as promised.

Later, with the tide at its full height, I paddled alone up Kapoose Creek. A few hundred yards along I passed through an invisible door into another world. All feeling of wind, sound of crashing surf, and sense of powerful sea vanished. The tall forest opened into a large, tranquil meadow. The creek carried not a ripple on its surface as it wound lazily through the thick, tall grass. The first hint of sunset's colours reflected in the calm waters, giving a perfect mirror image of the sky above. Everything was still.

I awoke about 2:00 AM. The wind still blew, but there was no sound of rain. I looked outside. Shadows stretched and danced on the sandy beach. Clouds sped quickly across the sky and now and then the light from the stars broke through.

In the morning, the wind continued and the sea looked rough. The sun hinted at its presence from behind an ever thickening layer of cloud. We decided to stay put and hope the "fast-moving front" would pass through in the next few days.

After a filling breakfast of hot porridge, we opted to spend the day hiking and looking about on foot. The tide was again extremely low, which allowed for wonderful exploration of pools, caves and islets normally surrounded by or under water. We'd not gone far when Mike, using his what I call "eyes that know what to look for," quietly said, "I bet it is."

"Bet it's what?" I asked.

"A burial cave," he replied.

It certainly wasn't obvious to the uninitiated eye. Slightly above us and set back under the trees was a hint of a black opening. Masses of large, vivid green ferns rose up in front of it. I clambered up behind Mike to a small ledge where I could now see the shallow cave mouth. I bent low and stepped inside. There was more than enough light entering from the outside to allow us to see quite clearly. Human bones lay on the cave floor, as did several hand-worked, cedar coffin planks. I wondered aloud whether animals or people had broken up the coffins and scattered the bones about.

"I'd like to think it was animals," said Mike. "But I wouldn't be surprised if humans haven't played a part in this, too." He recounted stories of other caves and burial islands he and paddling companions had come upon in their travels. Some had seemed perfectly intact, whereas others had obviously been ransacked by "trophy" hunters. It had been a sad experience for him to see such desecration.

"We kind of made it an unspoken rule to disturb nothing and to tell no one of the locations," he said.

We stayed awhile longer, standing still and letting our eyes wander. Then we quietly turned and stepped out into the bright day. From fifteen yards away I would never have taken a second glance at the narrow opening.

For me, finding the cave added another dimension to being out here. It allowed a veil to lift. Not enough for me to even come close to understanding or seeing, but to at least begin to get a tiny sense of a time and people who lived in these forests and plied these waters in their open canoes. A people whom I'm sure were at home with their sense of place in the larger scheme of things.

My sleep that night was interrupted by many strange dreams of which I could make little sense. Then, around 1:00 AM, I awoke to the sound of rain on the tarps. I climbed out and made sure everything was snug and under cover. When I next woke it was a little after 6:00, and the rain beat down steadily and the sky was dark. Still, it didn't look too bad. The sea appeared whitecapped, but not overly so. The wind was moderate and the tide was high enough to allow an easy exit almost from our doorstep. It was then that I saw Mike returning from the far end of the beach. He was already up and checking things out.

"It's a lot rougher out there than it appears from this corner. We're quite protected over here," he said.

"So, what do you think?" I asked.

"I don't know. Let's have breakfast and see what it looks like after that."

By the time we'd finished breakfast the sky looked even darker. We put on our rain gear and took a walk. When we reached the far end of the beach the full brunt of the south-easterly became evident. We talked. Mike thought it would probably be quite "lumpy" getting around Rugged Point. "Lumpy" was Mike's understated way of indicating we'd probably die or come close to it!

We spent the day walking well to the south. We could hear the faint sound of chainsaws being carried on the wind. Mike knew the logging plans for the area and told me that by this time next year all the adjacent forest would be gone. It was a depressing thought and one I could not fully absorb.

The light conditions were spectacular. Fast-moving clouds with dark squalls of mist and rain would suddenly break open, allowing shafts of brilliant sunlight to shine down. There were also periods of quiet and calm, broken by violent wind gusts which swept in like massive freight trains out of control.

That night, after a warm, filling, veggie-noodle stew, we listened to the updated forecast. The "fast-moving, intense low" had stalled. We could expect this same weather for many days to come. I fell asleep to the sound of pounding surf. A dense mist swirled over the beach and rain pelted down on the tarps. Everything was beginning to feel a *wee* bit damp.

In the morning there was no change. It was a miserably wet day with no sign of letup. The forecast indicated the front was moving very slowly with "intense rain, at times reducing visibility to zero." Gale-force winds were to continue. It was hard to tell the state of the sea from our camp. Fast-moving, large swells could be seen running in from the southeast, which would push us nicely in the right direction. Still, it was tough to assess standing on shore. Again Mike muttered, "It's probably quite lumpy out there."

We ate a hearty breakfast of pancakes, huddled under our kitchen tarp, and then decided we'd pack our gear and paddle out for a "look see." The creek was still at a good height, so we had only a short distance to carry the fully laden craft.

I was very nervous getting into my kayak. My adrenaline raced, my mouth seemed dry, and I could feel the pounding of my heart. I was dressed warmly for I was worried about becoming hypothermic. I knew we were going to get very wet, and with the winds, it would be a chilly time.

We paddled down the creek and pushed out through the surf into swells which were strong, despite the protection afforded us by nearby reefs. Once past these we were hit by the full force of the gale. Powerful seas came from the stern quarter. The only positive factor was that everything was generally going our way; otherwise, I could never have paddled any distance into those conditions.

The swell would roar in, lift my kayak, then occasionally break violently broadside, threatening to capsize me. Other times the breaking sea would slam the stern with such force that I'd instantly be knocked sideways. In either case, I often had to brace to stay upright. At one point a particularly steep wave lifted my bow well clear of the water, and a powerful blast of wind hit the exposed nose and threatened to flip me over. Fortunately, the combination of a heavily loaded boat and a quick brace saved the day.

Interestingly enough, fear did not rise up and over-whelm me, probably because there was simply too much energy required to pay attention, stay right side up, and make any progress. With each brace or backstroke I would slowly lose ground and drift closer to the lethal rock and reef along the shoreline. It was then necessary to turn and paddle seaward, but it was a vulnerable position to be in, as the swells then hurtled in on a broadside path. Added to this was the sudden presence of heavy rain squalls that greatly reduced visibility. It made for quite a ride.

Mike was a little ahead of me and to the right. From time to time I'd get a glimpse of his boat being slammed into a broadside position and his paddle being thrust out for a saving brace. Eventually we made it to Rugged Point and turned to round the treacherous headland. It was wild. On one of my backward glances, checking for breaking swells, I glimpsed the plunging bow of what appeared to be a government Fisheries vessel. I wondered if they were holding out there to see if we would make it to safety, for surely we must have looked like two matchsticks being tossed about. From my viewpoint, the Fisheries boat looked to be having an even more horrendous time than us. The bow would lift, then crash downwards, completely disap-pearing; then it'd slowly rise up, and incredible amounts of water would stream off the cabin and deck. Then down it'd go again.

We paddled intently and soon made it out of the cha-otic conditions into the mouth of Kyuquot Sound and around the corner into the protected waters of the cove. What a difference! We slid onto the shore through a gentle surf and crawled out, absolutely soaked, but warm, and glad to be alive. Mike summed it up in quiet tones, "That's the worst I've paddled in. We probably shouldn't have been out there."

The Fisheries boat went by, headed for a protected cove further along. We stood and drank copious amounts of water and munched on granola bars. The rain intensified and beat down with an incredible force. The drops literally seemed to machine-gun into the sand, then ricochet up and beat down a second time. Small streams poured out of the saturated forest and down the beach to the sea. We looked at each other — our resemblance to the proverbial drowned rat was too much to ignore, and we burst out laughing.

We waited for the rain squall to pass, then climbed into our kayaks and headed off down the Sound. Wind, swell, and current continued in our direction, moving us along nicely. We made good time the remaining eleven or so miles to Fair Harbour.

We drove to Campbell River that night, and next morning stopped at the Ministry of Forests office. They confirmed Mike's earlier forecast of extensive clearcut logging plans for the area behind and south of Kapoose. Most of it would be gone by the end of next year. We then further compounded our depression by going to the offices below to speak with the conservation officer. Our naive aim was to see whether bear, wolf, and bird habitat would have any value when stacked up against the plans of multi-national logging companies.

The officer was polite and pleasant. He stood talking with us, the heads of stuffed animals mounted on the walls around him. It soon became evident that we were wasting our time. A tree with an eagle's nest (many of which Mike had marked with tape while on our walks) might be spared, but all the rest would be cut. As for black bears, they were of little concern. In fact, it seemed there were already too many of them anyway, and thus there was no value placed on their habitat disruption. As for the wolves, not only was there no interest in protecting them, we were told the government had granted year-round open season on killing wolves. We found that our tax dollars were going to purchase traps, which would be provided free of charge to trappers.

It was a sobering conclusion to a memorable journey in such a wild and beautiful place.

BROKEN ISLANDS

BROKEN ISLANDS

〜〜〜

OVER THE YEARS I've tried to make a habit of joining Mike for a paddle out to the Broken Group every fall. This particular year we managed to get away in mid-October, and the drive from Victoria to Toquart Bay had taken us just over four hours. It was a warm, clear day. Stretched out before us lay over one hundred islands filling the eight-hundred-square-kilometre expanse of Barkley Sound. The sea was calm and there was little wind; t-shirts and sunglasses were the order of the day. It was hard to imagine this panorama by its other title: "The Graveyard of the Pacific" . . . so named for the many vessels that had sunk in its waters.

We loaded, launched, and paddled out past the Stopper Islands, over to St. Innes and then Bryant. We paused and I scanned the horizon with my binoculars, resting my gaze on Forbes Island.

"Do you remember the first time I came out here and we went over to Forbes?" I asked.

"Do I remember!" laughed Mike. . . .

~~~~~~

We'd been returning from a three-day paddle in the Broken Islands and had crossed Loudoun Channel to Forbes Island. On a whim I'd decided to attempt a landing through a narrow, rock-strewn opening onto a small beach. It was a wonderful example of how ignorant I still was at understanding and reading the situation.

I started in, on what I perceived to be a moderate wave. As the large volume of water was squeezed into the narrow passage, the swell quickly grew in size and speed! When Mike saw what I was up to, he shouted out, "I don't think that's a good idea!"

With paddle flailing I shot by on the ever-increasing swell and screamed in passing, "It's too late, I think I'm already committed!"

I was carried at what seemed an incredible speed into the channel, passing only inches above jagged rocks, and narrowly missing large boulders on my left and right. With great luck and minimal skill, I rode the back of the swell to the only soft landing spot available and managed to leap out, seconds after my bow slid up the steep beach. With a roar the surge sucked the remnants of my swell back, into the path of an even larger incoming wave. I turned to smile at Mike. He sat comfortably outside the mess and indicated he had no intention of joining me —wise man!

I took a quick look around, stopped for a well-needed pee, and then prepared to depart. It must have been comedy hour in the heavens, for the gods allowed me to exit unscathed, only to discover that I'd left my expensive sunglasses on the beach. Buoyed by my successful entrance and exit, I foolishly turned and climbed the back of the next incoming wave.

Things did not go so well this time.

I moved in too quickly, rising almost immediately to the top of the swell. I remember thinking, "If I stay in this position I shall land on the beach as gently as an over-ripe watermelon dropping on concrete!" I back-paddled frantically —too much so. The swell roared ahead and broke on the shore. I was now too far behind! By the time I neared the beach, the powerful surge grabbed me, stopped my forward motion, and sucked me backwards. I was swept off to the side and bumped into several friendly, round boulders. Only a short distance away stood some sharp-edged monsters that looked as though they ate fibreglass and bearded men for lunch. I was a goner if I got pulled out any further. I dumped the kayak on its side and abandoned ship. The water was bitterly cold, but fortunately only chest deep. I grabbed the toggle on the kayak's stern and pulled it like a reluctant dog shoreward. What could have been a dangerous situation had turned into a laughable one. Mike sat outside the channel, warm and dry, shaking his head in disbelief.

I finished bailing the water from my cockpit, then turned. My sunglasses sat innocently on a nearby log. I humbly reached out, picked them up, and put them on . . . then launched back into the surf and out to Mike.

My pride was soggy, but both craft and body had been spared injury and I'd been shown again how powerful the ocean was and how much I had to learn.

It was only minutes later, while paddling the calm waters off the north shore of Forbes, that a steep swell suddenly rose up behind Mike and snapped his kayak sideways. A wonderful reflex brace on his part prevented an almost certain capsize. We moved a slight distance away and paused to watch. Every few minutes a swell would rise up, indicating the shoal that lay below. Mike commented that if he hadn't practised his braces so much off Kapoose Beach, he'd surely have gone over.

I must be honest . . . it would have been wonderful to see him swept over, to see his gear floating about, to watch him struggle to re-enter, before I graciously paddled over to assist.

~~~~~

"Well, think I'll pass on going over to Forbes and showing you my superb surfing skill," I said.

Mike smiled.

We paddled on, making our way past Dodd and Willis islands, and slowly approached a couple of unnamed islets. The sun was hot. Mike's little keychain thermometer indicated over ninety degrees! We spied a fairly steep, white shell beach and altered course towards it. The water was a bright, clear green — almost turquoise.

The powerful open ocean could be sensed here. Though the cove was well protected, the sea's momentum carried the swell around the corner of the island, sending it to its final destination with a thunderous crash on adjacent rocks. We slid into the beach on a gentle surge and stepped out. Paradise. No one to be seen.

"A nice, cold beer would sure go down well right now," said Mike.

"Don't torment me," I replied.

He wandered off to take a pee and I stretched out, back against a log, to bask in the day's warmth. Mike came out of the trees and sat down beside me.

"Want a sip?" He handed me a cool beer — an *Anchor Steam* (from a small brewery in San Francisco), to be exact.

"What! Where'd you get this?"

It turned out that he'd been out here a few weeks earlier on one of his manic solo paddles, and upon leaving this little jewel of an islet he'd stashed a beer in the cool of the undergrowth for just such an occasion as this. How thoughtful!

We paddled on and Clarke Island came into view. I pulled out my binoculars, fully prepared to have to share this gem with others. No one. Just the magnificent, well-protected beach, with the little cabin off to the side and a pair of eagles perched high in a nearby tree. I couldn't believe our good fortune. We paddled in, pulled the kayaks up, then walked the short distance through the trees to an adjacent beach. There was no one there, either. We returned and set up camp on the sand. I angled my tent so the door opening would allow me to see both the midnight moon and the morning sunrise.

I paddled back out to a nearby reef and quickly caught a

couple of rockfish for dinner. The small fillets, poached in white wine, were exquisite. Alongside we had steamed broccoli, egg noodles, and firm, fresh tomatoes, with the ever-present assortment of spices. We ate on the adjacent beach, sipped a glass of wine, and watched the sun slowly sink into the ocean. A twisted pine, atop a rocky outcropping, stood silhouetted by the brilliant pinks of the setting sun.

I turned and walked back to my tent, gazing at the collage of soft colour reflected high in the sky. Movement down by the low tide caught my attention. I sat still and stared. Three small deer emerged from the chilly waters, apparently having swum the short distance from Owen Island. There was a horned buck, a doe, and a fawn. All three shook themselves vigorously, then faded into the evening darkness. I crawled into my tent, read awhile, then fell into a deep sleep.

The sound of an otter or mink alongside my tent woke me in the middle of the night. I looked out. A half moon hung in the star-filled sky and the beach appeared covered in a blanket of soft, white snow. Much later, I awoke and watched the sky shift from vibrant orange to pink, then to fading pastels, as the sun lifted up over the distant mountains. I could hear the sound of Mike's VHF radio coming from his tent. The voice called for clouds, rain, and impending storms. I looked outside again. No wind; clear blue sky.

After a breakfast of scrambled eggs, sourdough bread, and coffee, we paddled over to Benson Island and drifted along the shoreline. The sun filtered through the treetops, filling an inner meadow with soft morning light. Shadows moved silently, then bent their heads. One, then another, moved into the clearing. They were deer. Only in kayaks could we slip up this close, observe, then slide away unnoticed.

We rounded the corner of Benson, wove through some reef, and then headed for the outermost islet, Sail Rock. As we approached, a lone eagle could be seen atop the highest crag. Even on a calm day such as this, the power of the incoming swell was intimidating. There was nothing to break or slow the momentum. Beyond lay only open ocean. Next stop, Japan.

Mike pulled alongside and told me how on a past occasion he and friends, Philip and Stephanie, had paddled out here on a stormy day. The feeling had been quite different — "menacing" was the word he used. It confirmed what I'd felt time and time again. When the sun shone, wild and dangerous conditions took on an exhilarating challenge; when the sky turned grey and dark, and the wind begin to howl, then fear would often creep in and a menacing atmosphere would indeed seem prevalent.

Today, the sun continued its course in a cloudless sky and the wind slept. We paddled slowly around Sail Rock, admiring its rugged beauty. On the far side stretched an almost endless swath of brilliant white foam. As we paddled into it, the only comparison that came to mind was of walking in a fresh, deep snowfall. All sound seemed absorbed. Waves reared and came down on rocks a short distance away, yet virtually no sound reached my ears. Further on, the solid white sheet had broken into a million pieces — as though golden white blossoms had been cast adrift on the ocean's surface.

We paddled on, taking general aim for Wouwer Island. We stayed well clear of Verbeke Reef, where the swells climbed upon themselves until they toppled and crashed violently. Mike suddenly shouted and I turned to look where he pointed. About one hundred yards away, out to sea, a wall of water rose up the height of a two-storey house — there must be a rock or reef out there! It failed to break and we were simply lifted up as it moved quickly under and past.

I looked again, and saw that about seventy-five yards from Mike a great hole had been opened in the sea by the passing swell. The next wave exploded in the crater, and with a wild confusion of white and deep-green all evidence of the cavernous opening vanished. My heart pounded but the swells that followed were only moderate. I recalled a little pamphlet put out by the government. It noted that statistically every twelve hundredth wave could be expected to be twice the size of the average height of the highest one-third of the waves. I guess number twelve hundred had just passed through. It had been huge.

We paddled on and soon heard the sound of sea lions in the distance. A short while later we entered the channel between Wouwer and Batley Islands, where some two hundred or more of these creatures seemed spread everywhere. Mammoth Stellar sea lions, perched high on the rocks, stretched their swollen necks, arched, postured, and gave forth with deep, vibrant roars, truly like their jungle-lion namesakes. Below them, California sea lions barked and frolicked. A gigantic head suddenly rose one and a half feet from my bow, turned and only *just* slid under my hull! Another twenty-five or so lay in the water off to my right, apparently at some form of yoga class, for their postures appeared inverted and contorted, with only tails or single flippers rising above the surface.

As we moved further into the channel, the echoing chorus of sound became almost deafening. We stuck to the middle of the passage, having sensed an invisible territorial line for those on the rocks. Cross the line and the roars and activity increased markedly. Heads pointed directly at us; huge bodies shifted and prepared to launch themselves from great heights into the sea. Back-paddle, exit over the invisible line, and all settled to the proverbial dull roar.

Their speed and agility in the water was astounding. Some, in groups of eight or ten, would swim directly at us, then dive and pass underneath. Not only could I see them in the clear water, but I could *feel* their vocals reverberate through my feet!

We moved slowly on, and while still on the protected side of Wouwer Island came upon our first kayakers — four of them. One of the men announced that it was a shame there were no sea lions about. Mike and I stared incredulously, for even here their sound was loud. We drew his attention to this, but he continued to insist there were only a few. We smiled and paddled on through the narrow opening between Wouwer and an unnamed islet, into exposed waters. We paused and plotted a course through the rocks and boomers, and then made our way to a well-protected little cove. We hauled the kayaks up a safe distance, unpacked our lunch, and headed for the exposed edge of Wouwer.

The ground over which we walked appeared at first glance to be a desolate moonscape, with no sign of life. Upon closer examination, however, I saw a miniworld of articulate beauty . . . little pools and soft patches of grass and moss, sprinkled here and there with tiny wildflowers of all colours. There were several lone bonsai gripping naked rock. Stunted shore pine, bordering the area, leaned away from the ocean at wickedly steep angles, a testament to the severity of the storms that lashed these shores.

We climbed the last steep rock, sat, and looked down a short distance to where the incoming sea met the island. The swell would roar in, rise up, and explode, smothering the rock with white and swirling green. Then with equally dramatic power the surge would suck back, suddenly dropping the water level twenty or thirty feet, exposing new worlds of rock and pools. Then "BOOM!" and the next swell would explode, fill the empty spaces, and crawl even higher up the cliff where we sat, contentedly munching our lunch.

The sun continued to beat down; the day's heat was remarkable for October. So much so that by the time we returned to Clarke it took little impetus to strip and dive into the brisk ocean waters for an invigorating "bath." Later I stretched out on the white shell beach and drifted off.

A light scrunching sound to my near left woke me. I lay still, opened my eyes, and stared at a small deer less than five feet away. Like her cousins of the previous night, this one was wet and had obviously crossed over the short distance from Owen Island. The doe shook herself and I could feel the drops land on my skin. I moved; she turned and bounded off. I closed my eyes and again sank into the warmth and softness of the day.

Next morning the sun rose in a clear, deep-blue sky,

despite the continued forecast of cloud, wind, and inclement weather. We moved slowly —while eating breakfast, in dismantling our tents, and loading our gear. There was a reluctance to head homeward.

Eventually we launched and slipped into the calm waters. We chose a return journey almost twice the distance our route out. We wove around countless islands and through myriad winding waterways. In the end we could no longer postpone the inevitable and turned towards Toquart Bay.

I hoped some of this would come home with me . . . and perhaps stay awhile.

NIGHT WHISTLE

NIGHT WHISTLE

MIKE AND I were headed for a camp on the south end of the Brooks Peninsula, not far from Cape Cook and Solander Island. I was very tired! Over the past two days we had paddled some forty-five miles with kayaks fully loaded for a three-week journey, and it seemed we'd been constantly beating into a headwind.

Despite the exhaustion, I felt quite exhilarated. It had long been a dream of mine to spend time here. Although clearcut logging scars were now outrageously evident up and down the west coast of Vancouver Island, the Brooks Peninsula remained intact. There was no road access and sailing guides warned mariners to keep well clear of the dangerous rock and reef that covered the shoreline. Cape Cook is known as the "Cape of Storms," and we'd heard tales of hurricane winds sweeping over Solander Island, seizing up wind speed indicators at over one hundred and twenty knots. The wild and rugged nature of the area had been further enhanced with a uniqueness of flora and fauna, as much of the Brooks had apparently escaped the direct impact of the last ice age. It was truly one of the few pristine coastal wilderness areas left.

We pulled into the rock-strewn cove with little difficulty and landed on a massive pile of drying seaweed that gently cushioned our arrival. Logs could be seen lying deep in the forest, evidence of the powerful southeast winds that lashed this coast in the winter. For now, the prevailing northwesterlies of summer allowed us to camp in relative calm. The beach was a combination of sand and large rocks, set on a steep angle. It took us ages to prepare two level sites for the tents.

Clouds scudded rapidly by and our VHF radio told of twenty-five- to thirty-knot northwest winds off Solander. Here, it was well protected and calm. We hoped the winds would drop in the next day or two, allowing us a chance to head out and around the Cape to the north side of the Brooks.

We ate a good supper and noticed the clouds slowing their pace to a crawl. A commercial fishboat approached, then stopped and set anchor outside our bay. The sun disappeared behind the Peninsula and a full moon rose in the sky. I crawled into bed feeling delightfully tired. I called out to Mike, "If you get up in the middle of the night and the moon looks particularly good, call me. Okay?"

"Sure. No problem."

I was awakened around 3:00 AM by Mike's voice. "You should have a look. It's really quite beautiful."

The design of my tent would not allow me to easily look out and see the moon. I lay warm and sleepy, and pondered. Ah well, maybe I would take a pee as well. I unzipped the door and struggled out. Mike had returned to his tent.

I stood naked and alone in a magical landscape. The

full moon, appearing larger than I'd ever seen, hung suspended in a star-studded sky. A silver path fell from it and lay across the water, stretching up the beach to my feet. The sand appeared coated in sparkling dust. The sea was flat, and the fishboat lay quietly at anchor. Way out on the ocean, at the earth's curve, lights twinkled faintly — a fishing fleet, balanced on the edge of the world. There was no wind. All was profoundly still and soft in the moonlight.

It's moments like this that stay etched in the mind and heart. For a short period the conscious mind lets go, an awareness slips in, and you are simply a part of something much larger and more mysterious than your mind will ever comprehend.

I knelt and crawled back into my tent. I settled into the warmth of the old down bag and closed my eyes. Minutes later Mike whispered from his tent, "Quick! Take a look!"

But I was sleepy, content.

"Why?" I eventually replied.

"There's a wolf out there."

My mind refused to accept this. It was too perfect. A wolf walking across a silver beach under a full moon on a jewel of a night such as this!

"Are you sure?" I whispered back.

"Too late, I think it's gone," he said quietly.

As I drifted off, a last thought came to me. *If* there really had been a wolf out there, it must have been watching me when I was standing naked in the moonlight!

Then peaceful, deep, deep sleep.

~~~~~

Just after dawn I stirred, then slept awhile longer. Eventually I crawled out. Mike was already up.

"Now what's this about a wolf?" I asked.

Mike sat on a log, lacing up his running shoes. "I was lying awake in bed when I thought I heard a sound like a high, sharp whistle," he said. "So I looked out and there was a wolf moving across the beach — moving quite quickly in that direction," and he pointed off to our left.

I put on my shoes and we walked over to the far edge

of our beach. To my surprise, we immediately found not one but two large sets of very fresh wolf tracks. These definitely had *not* been here yesterday. We followed them across the sand and into rock and seaweed, picking them up again on the other side. My eyes stared incredulously. The tracks approached to within twenty feet of my tent, then veered and headed down towards the tide line. They eventually vanished into the rocky outcropping on the other side of the bay.

"It was the whistle-like sound that caught my attention and caused me to look out," said Mike. "It sounded almost human."

We both sat quietly, deep in thought. For awhile I inwardly groaned and moaned at having not looked out when Mike had called. But that soon vanished, and I sat in wonder at being in a place so wild that something like this was even possible.

"Maybe there's a mythical spirit that walks with the wolves at night under the full moon," I conjectured. "Maybe that was who whistled . . . it was Wolf-Woman with her two guardians."

Mike smiled. "Maybe. . . . "

It was easy to let the dimensions of reality soften.

Mike and I have returned to the Brooks Penisula many times since that night, to both the north and south sides. Neither of us has ever heard the whistle again, but we've often found fresh wolf tracks. And each time we kneel beside them looking carefully for any sign of a ghostly imprint that might tell of Wolf-Woman's passing in the night with her four-legged guardians.

CRYSTAL BALLS AND RAINBOWS

CRYSTAL BALLS AND RAINBOWS

WE PACKED OUR gear and launched into the waters off the southwest side of the Brooks Peninsula. The early-morning weather report had nailed the lid shut on our plans to round Cape Cook. Already winds up to thirty-five knots blew out of the north, making it impossible for us to contemplate getting around the notorious "Cape of Storms." We turned and headed in the opposite direction, along the coast towards the Acous Peninsula. The high land mass of the Brooks protected us from the main on-slaught of the wind, although sporadic blasts would sweep down through some of the valleys and strike with surpris-ing force. It was a hot, late summer day. Now and then a batch of large white clouds would appear and race across an otherwise clear, blue sky. We moved at a lazy pace, ex-ploring the shoreline closely and enjoying the luxury of not having to paddle *into* the wind.

Rounding a large, rocky outcrop, we came upon an exquisite, crescent-shaped bay. The surf rolled in at a good clip and dumped with a resounding roar on the white sandy beach.

"You want to try landing first?" Mike politely asked.

"Naw . . . I hate showing off. I know how miserable you feel when you see the depth of my skill!"

We paused outside the surf zone; I glanced backwards, checking for any possible surprises, while Mike scanned the shore for a potential landing site.

"There might be an opening over there, to the left of the creek mouth by those big rocks," he suggested.

We watched closely as the swells rose, then turned into the corner Mike had pointed out. Much of their energy was lost in taking the turn, and those that broke did so in a much milder fashion than elsewhere on the beach.

"If we catch the right set of waves, we could probably make it in without much trouble," said Mike.

"We've got to stay away from those rocks . . . the ones over there." I pointed to a collection of partially submerged, nasty looking specimens. Mike nodded.

A large and powerful sequence of swells approached and we back-paddled, staying well outside the break line. They swept through and then there was a noticeable calm. A smaller wave passed under us, then an even smaller one. We both glanced behind. "Let's go!" I shouted. We dug hard and the swells that followed were moderate and well spaced, allowing us ample time to make our way in and land safely.

We hauled the kayaks above the high tide line, then grabbed the water bags and headed up the nearby creek. There had been little rain in recent months, and the lower water level allowed us to easily follow the creek's course deeper and deeper into the forest. Rounding a bend, I suddenly stopped. In front of me, the full force of the creek cascaded over a sheer precipice, then plunged into a seemingly bottomless pool. The sunlight filtered through the towering trees and cast a thousand sparkling diamonds upon the water's surface. The floating mist picked them up and formed a delicate, soft rainbow.

I walked to the edge of the pool, stripped, and plunged into the icy waters.

"Oh, my God, but it's cold!"

I quickly washed the dirt and grime from my body, dove under once more, then scrambled onto a large rock in the centre of the creek. My skin tingled; my heart pounded. I squatted, pulled my knees against my chest, and closed my eyes. There was only the roar of the creek, the bracing scent of cool, fresh air, and the pervading sun's warmth through my naked body. It was an uncluttered, refreshingly simple moment.

Later, I climbed back into my clothes and retraced my steps, eventually catching up with Mike, who stood at the edge of a beautiful pool; a pebble beach in front of him sloped quickly downward to a depth of some fifteen feet.

"Going to have a bath?" I asked.

"My clothes could do with a rinse as well," he laughed.

Without further ado he walked into the chilly waters, fully clothed, until he stood chest deep.

"Don't move!" I said. "Let me get my camera so I can record your baptismal rites."

I pulled out my small Olympus and clicked off several shots while Mike stood immersed, hands held high in prayer-like fashion. Then he did a few "washing machine" swirls and exited rapidly from the frigid waters. By the time we reached the mouth of the creek, the combination of synthetic clothing and hot sun had him almost perfectly dry.

The roar from the shore was noticeably louder; the wind and sea had obviously picked up as the day worn on. The surf was larger, faster and more destructive — especially for little boats. We carried the heavy kayaks to the water's edge, then stood and weighed the scene with justifiable apprehension. When instruction books describe launching in surf, they usually talk of small and empty craft, designed for white water or surf. They rarely discuss the challenge of entering chaos such as this in a fully loaded ocean kayak.

(Probably because you're supposed to be intelligent enough to not have landed here in the first place.)

It was our habit to take turns launching into dicey seas such as these. It was a nice luxury to have someone hold your craft in place while you fastened your spray skirt and then were propelled into the surf with a good shove. As my luck would have it, it was Mike's turn to go first. We moved his boat into the shallows. It required both of us to hold the heavy monster in place. Because we were at the corner of the beach, the waves did not roll in perpendicular to the shore; instead they came sideways, then swirled and struck from different angles. The tendency was for the water to grab the bow, turn the craft broadside and then sweep it into shore . . . the wave trying its utmost to dump into the exposed cockpit.

"Okay. It's looking calmer," said Mike.

"Go!" I barked.

Mike leapt in. We took a second glance. It definitely seemed a smaller set of waves was in progress. Not wasting time to fasten his spray skirt, he grabbed his paddle and dug in. I took the stern and pushed as hard as I could, running a short distance into the sea.

"Go! Go! Go!" I shouted. My whole body urged him on.

His paddle churned and he fairly flew along. Then a slightly larger wave appeared, rising towards him. He paddled fiercely, lifted up and over; the wave crashed downwards only a few seconds later. Mike was safe and dry. He paddled a short distance further, then turned to sit and watch my efforts at escape. He laughed and waved.

I dragged my boat into the water. Before I had time to look up, I found myself in the dangerous position of being between it and the shore. A wave slammed the bow, knocking it sideways, and I was nearly mowed under as the kayak was forced up the beach. I waited until a smaller set of waves appeared, then dragged the loaded beast back into the shallows. Now I faced the dual task of trying to keep the boat at right angles to the sea while getting into the cockpit. I was two-thirds in when I looked up and saw I was too late. A larger set of waves was on its way. I leapt out and pulled the craft back. I waited what seemed a long time before I sensed the first hint of a decrease in wave size. Again I quickly dragged the kayak into the water and flung myself into the cockpit. I looked up . . . things were so-so. "He who hesitates dies!" I thought. Then I paddled as fast as I could; no time to fasten my spray skirt. I made it over one wave, then another. Only one more to go . . . but it was rearing up, up! In slow motion my bow pierced the sharp peak of the swell; water rolled across the deck, coming closer and closer; now up to the cockpit coning; and then, with a last gasp, it slid over the top and dumped full into my lap, filling the cockpit with a good four to six inches of water.

"Arghhhhhh!" I screamed. I was soaked.

But I was out! I paddled a short distance further, then stopped. I took my hand pump, emptied out the water, and mopped up the dregs with a big sponge.

Mike paddled over. "Better you than me," he grinned.

"Two seconds faster and I'd have beaten it," I moaned.

Fortunately it was a warm day, and despite the increasing wind I was really quite comfortable. I fastened the spray skirt and we paddled on to the entrance of Nasparti Inlet. We guessed the outflow winds to be at about thirty knots; they would hit us directly on our port beam while we made the crossing. Huge white clouds had built directly on the ridge of the Brooks Peninsula and we could now see them spilling down the mountainsides into the valleys, as smoothly as an overflowing vanilla milkshake.

"You ready?" asked Mike.

I nodded affirmatively.

It was a wonderful, energetic crossing, full of breaking seas, fun, and challenge — absolutely exhilarating. Again I'm convinced that the lack of fog and the brightness of a warm, friendly sun made all the difference in my attitude. Had there been mist moving in and dark clouds blackening the sky, I swear my fear level would have been ten times higher.

After a brief nap on a protected shore we headed out to

the Cuttle Islets off the Acous Peninsula and soon found ourselves back in the full force of the increasing winds. This time they came from our stern, so we rafted the kayaks together and held up a small plastic tarp Mike carried. It acted as a wonderful sail and we roared along at a great clip, with white water peeling off the cutting edge of our bows. Before long, however, we were into dangerous waters with submerged rocks and exploding seas, all tied together with thick beds of kelp. We quickly lowered sail, pushed apart, and set to paddling a safe course.

In short time we landed on a lovely little beach on the outermost islet. The wind was now screaming along, whipping the clouds into magical formations, like a huge beater stirring up immense piles of meringue. We found an ideal site for our tents above the high tide line, well protected by a steep rock cliff upon which the islet's dense forest grew.

Later, having set up camp, I pushed out into the gale again and swung around to the more protected side of the islet and tied my craft to the edge of a large kelp bed. The protection was not all I would have wished. The wind whipped across the water's surface like the feet of a thousand ethereal dancers urging my kayak to break free and run with them. I made sure I was well fastened, having no desire to be blown into the main stream of the wind. I set up my little collapsible fishing rod and in short time had caught two sea trout. In less than fifteen minutes the four fillets were cooking in a hot skillet. That's what you call *fresh* fish.

After dinner the wind died completely, and we climbed the rocky cliff and forged our way through the islet's thick undergrowth to the western side. Here we sat and watched the brilliant sun slowly sink behind the Brooks, creating a sky of vibrant pinks. On the opposite horizon the moon rose slowly.

I sipped a glass of Cointreau. What more could a mere mortal ask?

After a hearty breakfast of "Sheehan Pancakes" (secret mix plus blueberries, lemon juice, and maple sugar crystals), we paddled over to one of the adjacent islets where several mature eagles sat in craggy treetops. At the forest's edge bleached human bones could be seen, mixed in amongst the shell and stone. Inland we found further evidence of human remains, including skulls, now partially covered in a deep green moss. In the thick undergrowth I could also discern what appeared to be hand-hewn planks. It was obviously a Native burial site. We touched and moved nothing, then turned and walked back to our kayaks.

As in the past when we had come upon burial caves, I was profoundly struck by the hint of a way of life in such contrast to my own. I thought of expensive, plush-lined coffins, accompanied by mammoth headstones etched deeply with names and dates, all created in an effort to ward off the inevitable ravages of time. Attempts at immortality, even in death. Here, it appeared that the bodily remains had been placed in the environment in which they had lived, and like all other things, would slowly dissolve back into their origin.

Later, on the Acous Peninsula, we stood on the site of an old Native village and marvelled at what is probably one of the last standing totems in the area. Mike and I talked of what it must have been like to have lived here hundreds of years ago, before the coming of the white man. Before the forests and creatures of both land and sea had been so decimated by man's seemingly insatiable need to conquer and destroy.

We paddled on, into the quiet of Battle Bay. A black bear walked the beach, then, sensing our presence, moved quickly on and disappeared into the forest. A fin broke the water close to Mike, then a second.

"Porpoise!" he cried out. We watched carefully but did not see them rise again.

We pulled into the bay and discovered recent wolf tracks alongside those of the bear. In the nearby creek, river otters splashed and disappeared. We sat and munched on some cheese and crackers, then returned to our craft. In the near distance we could see some kayaks pulled up against a rocky shore. We angled over and found four people trying to ladle water from the tiniest of rivulets into a half-litre container.

"We're really low on water," one of them said. We pulled out a chart and Mike made some suggestions about a better water source further along the shore, but they decided to continue on as they were. We wished them well and moved on, into the beginnings of Ououkinsh Inlet. We found a little bay, complete with a sparkling stream that rushed down the mountainside, over glistening rocks and into the sea.

"I think we should wait for that fellow to move on," said Mike quietly.

I turned my head to where he was looking. A large black bear ambled slowly along, across the sandy curve of the tiny cove. The breeze was offshore; we sat still and apparently went unnoticed. Later we filled our water containers, then turned and headed back to our campsite. Before we'd reached the half-way point the wind had picked up to a typical afternoon howl, and an arduous paddle was required before we finally touched the protected shore of our special islet.

After dinner we listened to the forecast, which told of impending gale- to storm-force winds and heavy rain. We decided to head through the Bunsby Islands the next day and down to either Lookout or Spring Island.

We were up at sunrise, ate, then packed and launched. Wind and current were at our backs and a stiff breeze fairly hurled us along towards the calm waters of the Bunsby Islands. In less than twenty-five minutes we reached Green Head Rock, standing prominently above reef and confused seas, and paddled into the tranquil waters on the backside of Checkaklis Island. Not a soul to be seen! A sea otter lay contentedly on its back, basking in a nearby bed of kelp.

We paddled through the Bunsbys and over to the Vancouver Island shore where the barren slopes of Mt. Paxton rose up, clearcut from bottom to top. This is the clearcut deemed so ugly that *National Geographic* magazine printed it as a glaring example of the poor logging and forestry management practices in our corner of the world.

We soon sensed the weather turning and stopped to chart a course that would involve a five-mile crossing to Lookout Island.

"This is definitely going to be a little damp," I said, "and I'm not talking about rain."

Mike nodded, "It looks like it could get *lumpy* alright."

We took turns steadying the other's kayak while we went through the ritual of removing the life jacket, digging out and putting on the paddling jacket, refastening the spray skirt, and finally donning the life jacket again. We both pulled toques on for good measure and then munched a couple of granola bars.

"Well, let's get going," said Mike, and off we moved.

Before getting a quarter of the distance we found ourselves in strong winds and rough seas, the sky a menacing grey. Waves broke with great regularity on the kayaks and before long we both looked like we'd showered with our clothes on. I was glad we'd had the foresight to put on the paddling jackets. We'd have been chilled through and through if we hadn't.

We pushed along and it got rougher; wind gusts continually tried to wrench the paddle from my hands. At times the seas rose up into sharp walls and my kayak would blast through, become momentarily airborne, then crash into the trough below with a sickening *bang*. My mind went back to stories I'd heard of poorly made kayaks, which when dropped had quite literally split in half along the lateral seam. I offered a brief prayer that those involved in the manufacture of my particular craft had been been extra diligent in their work!

Despite the gale-force winds we faced, Mike pulled steadily ahead. Between the high seas and ever deepening valleys, he would often disappear from sight for what seemed to be a substantial period of time. Then I'd catch a glimpse of him, holding steady, waiting for me to catch up. It was sensible kayaking and much appreciated.

Somehow, *not* being alone gave me a deep sense of well-being, even though I realized that in these conditions neither of us would be of much help in saving the other should a capsize occur. It was enough simply having the other person there. I recalled a former teacher telling me of being lost and alone in the jungle in the middle of the night, and how the fear had become almost paralysing. Later, upon finding his companion, he felt much, much better. Ironically, he was still in the jungle, still lost, and it was still dark, but somehow not being alone had altered things. Now I understood the feeling; in my case it somehow transformed a possible nightmare into a demanding adventure.

I pulled alongside. Mike grinned through rivulets of salt water running down his face. "How are you doing?"

"Not bad. The boat's amazing the way it handles things. I'm sure glad we're not having to paddle *into* this."

Mike agreed.

I confessed my fear. "I'd be scared to death if I was out here by myself."

"So would I," said Mike. "Wouldn't have come across by myself with the weather like this."

I was stunned! What a wonderfully honest statement.

We paddled on and before long found ourselves off Lookout Island. The incoming seas, combined with the steep beach, made it a poor time to consider landing, so we decided "maybe tomorrow," and headed across the channel to a well-protected cove on the outside of Spring Island. We landed, and, to our delight, found no one about. We worked for awhile at clearing two sites and a kitchen area. Rain looked imminent, so we strung up a variety of tarps to ensure as much dryness as possible.

To celebrate surviving our paddle in the gale, we went whole hog in cooking up a "Mexican Night Dinner": tortillas, refried beans, hot chilies, cheese, tomatoes, onions, hot sauce, and chilled wine. On our menu rating scale of 0 to 10 I gave it a 9.9.

That night the skies opened and aimed their heavenly fire hose directly upon us. I fell asleep to the sound of beating rain and the tinkle of streams of water flowing off the tarps into strategically placed pots.

~~~~~

In the morning, massive white clouds, with perfectly straight bottoms, filled the sky. Now and then the sun would break through and steam would rise from wherever its warmth struck the shore. By the time we'd finished breakfast there were huge blue openings in the sky and it looked more and more like a good day ahead. We walked along a nearby beach, stopped, and peered through our binoculars at the shore of Lookout Island.

"We might be able to land today," said Mike.

"Possible, but tricky," I answered. "Let's flip a coin to see who has to go in first." Mike lost. I looked up to the gods and smiled, "Thank you, thank you."

My eye suddenly caught a glimpse of a strange, green something, well above the tide line. I turned towards it; Mike continued to walk along the fresh path of kelp and debris laid down by this morning's high tide. As I got closer I saw that my *special something* was in fact a green garbage bag wrapped around a broken plastic bottle.

"Well, well, well," I heard Mike say. I turned and saw him bend over. "Never found one this big."

"What've you got?" I asked in anxious tones. After all, if I'd only kept walking instead of pursuing garbage bags, I would have been the one to stumble on the *find*.

He pivoted in my direction. In his hands lay a gleaming, dark-green, Japanese glass float, the size of a soccer ball. Somehow this gem had come in from the Pacific Ocean, through countless islets, rock, and reef, to roll up intact on this very beach at the moment of our choosing to go for a walk. What a find! Twenty yards in front of me, and I'd gone chasing garbage bags instead. "My day's ruined," I muttered.

~~~~~

We packed a lunch and paddled over to Lookout Island. Mike assessed a possible landing spot and at the critical moment sprinted for shore, caught the swell at the right height and angle, and was carried softly up onto the beach. Then the surge sucked down the incline and out. Mike removed his spray skirt at what seemed to be a painfully slow speed as his kayak started sliding down the steep slope on the ball-bearing pebbles. At the last possible moment he stepped out, grabbed the bow toggle, and walked forward as the incoming swell caught the stern and pushed the kayak along with him. Well done! Poetry in motion.

The critical window was much wider for me. When I arrived on the beach, Mike simply grabbed my bow toggle, thus giving me ample time to unfasten the spray skirt and exit, with no fear of being sucked back into the vortex.

The tide was well out, making it easy to explore the island's circumference. I found Japanese *plastic* floats, complete with Oriental script, and thick pieces of dark green, curved glass, indicative of fishing floats that had survived their Pacific journey only to be dashed to smithereens on the rocks. But nowhere could my eyes glimpse an intact glass ball.

Inland, all was quiet and peaceful. Large Sitka spruce rose up, with serene meadows of tall grass spaced between them — a marked difference from the normal dense underbrush of the west coast. Thick green moss covered whole sides of trees and hung like plush robes on extended branches. At the foot of one tree we found the skeleton of an eagle, its distinct plumage lying around it. Tiny feathers of other birds dotted the ground at the entrance to small underground burrows, betraying their occupants. We walked softly, carefully. Shafts of sunlight filtered down, in stark contrast to the dark, towering spruce. It would not have seemed out of place had a deep voice suddenly spoken out of the light. The word "magical" aptly described the feeling. We wandered off in different directions, each lost in his own inner world. "If my time had come," I thought, "this would be a fine place in which to lay my weary bones."

Some time later I came across Mike, back on the southern shore. To my right, a hundred yards or more of sharp, black rock stretched to the water's edge. On my left was a long row of logs, piled almost two storeys high.

"Can you imagine the power of the storms?" Mike said. Enormous logs lay imbedded in the forest floor, with dozens of equal size jammed on top. He bent down and started to pull out a round, dark green item.

"No! Not another," I groaned.

"No," he laughed. "It's a bottle of champagne!" Alas, the contents had been contaminated by salt water, but it did set us to looking in the ten million possible nooks and crannies in the log jumble.

I reached in, and down. My fingers touched something cool and smooth. My heart leapt. "Relax, it's probably just a bottle," I thought. I pulled out a light-green, gloriously intact Japanese glass fishing float, the size of a small orange. "I found one! I found one!" I beamed from ear to ear like a little child. It was as though I'd found a magic crystal ball. I looked out across the hundred yards of wicked rock. The glass ball's tiny size made it seem all the more vulnerable and special. How did it make it across those rocks and then slide safely into its little hole and not get crushed by these giant logs?

We continued to prowl about for several hours and in the end found a total of eleven glass floats, all varying in size, shape, and colour. We played like children in a sandbox, totally absorbed in our search, and more than satisfied with the discovery of our simple treasures.

Later, we wandered back through the cool, sunlit shadows of the interior, to the beach where we'd left the kayaks. After lunch I volunteered to try and catch a salmon for dinner. The time of day was totally wrong, but I'd seen some of the Natives from Kyuquot trying their luck in the somewhat turbulent channel between Lookout and Spring and thought it worth a shot. Mike helped launch me successfully into the surf, then he returned to the forest to take more photographs.

I paddled out and over to a spot where reef and kelp gave way to a deeper channel. The incoming northwest swells seemed to wrap around Lookout and clash at this point, not only with themselves, but also with the current. The seas were confused and flecked with white foam. It seemed a vibrant spot. Gulls cried and dove madly into schools of feed. A commercial troller came through, slowed, and left its gear out. "Must be a good place," I thought. My kayak bobbed on the surface, like a little cork. I was alert for surprises, but all in all, things seemed well under control. I pulled out my little fishing rod and began.

I was on my third cast when the ocean bulged about thirty yards away. I stared but saw nothing. Then a fin broke the water not ten feet in front of me. I dropped the rod and grabbed my camera. Too late. Then the water opened up about fifteen yards to my right and the large dark back and small fin of what looked to be a minke whale appeared. Click. Got my picture; proof for the story that would be told later. My heart pounded with excitement at the closeness of it all.

The whale cruised about for some time, but never came as close again, and eventually I lost sight of it. The afternoon winds began making my ride much bumpier, especially with the kayak being empty, and I decided to pass on further fishing. I turned and headed back to camp, relishing the event I had just experienced.

We packed the next day but didn't enter Kyuquot Sound until almost noon. By that time the winds were blowing a strong but comfortable twenty-five knots at our backs, with mild seas. We paddled and surfed our loaded craft at a great clip, with little fear of broaching. We horsed about, trying to use everything from tarps to tent flies, as sails. We were having so much fun that it was not until we reached the mouth of the Tahsish Inlet that we suddenly noticed the dramatic decrease in temperature. I turned and looked up the inlet. Coming around the corner, out of the blue sky, was the blackest of black squalls. I could see the torrential rains beating on the water. A line seemed drawn across the surface, and it moved rapidly towards us, closer and closer. The sound of driving rain increased to a roar.

"It's going to get us before we get to the truck," shouted Mike. Fair Harbour, where our vehicle was parked, lay a good two miles away.

The contrast between bright, sunlit sky and absolute darkness turned the inlet into a world of shadowy spirits. We turned and paddled for all we were worth; the roar of pounding rain closed in.

We both suddenly looked up, our paddles slowed, then stopped; we stared in awe. A brilliant rainbow stretched in all its vibrant glory from one side of the Tahsish Inlet to the other. Then, above it, a softer, subtler one appeared. It was stunning in its beauty. Gone was the urge to beat the squall. It was a lost race anyway.

The drumbeat of the rain swept over us; the rainbows faded, then were gone. Within minutes we were drenched; the abundance of fresh water turned our hands into ancient-looking prunes.

No matter we were soaked, it had been a grand day. And I found there was truth in the saying: "No rain, no rainbows."

THE LAGOON

THE LAGOON

WE DROVE FROM Port McNeill to Port Alice, then a further three hours on logging roads, and eventually arrived at the northern side of Klaskino Inlet. The drive from Port Alice was not uplifting. Visible everywhere were endless clearcuts, slash and burn areas, and landslide after landslide descending from the logging roads.

Mike was far more knowledgeable than I about the effects of our present logging and reforestation practices. As a result we were constantly stopping while he made a point or took a photograph.

In Port McNeill we had enquired at the forest company's office about travelling on the logging roads and had been assured there were no trucks moving on our route. It soon became obvious that the Port McNeill office and the field operations were not going to win the communication award of the year. On several occasions we assumed the world was about to end —the ground seemed to move, a deafening roar approached, and the sun's light dimmed as the sky filled with dust. Then, around the corner, barrelling down upon us, would loom a fully loaded logging truck, filling the entire width of the road. Fortunately, Mike's vehicle was a four-wheel drive and he simply dove for the safest ditch he could find while the beast roared by. After a short time the sky would clear and we'd move on, our paranoia in full bloom.

Eventually we rounded Redstripe Mountain, which was in the process of being clearcut from bottom to top, and gazed out upon the beauty of Klaskino Inlet. In the distance lay the wild, exposed, northern side of the Brooks Peninsula, with peak after peak reaching almost three thousand feet into the heavens.

It was a hot August day. The forecast was for a building high with northwest winds of thirty-five to forty knots. Even from our position well above the inlet we could see the strong lines of incoming swell. A cap of cloud sat perched on the distant peninsula. Sailing books warned that when the "cap was on the Cape," strong winds and rough seas could be expected; rounding the Cape was then best left for another day.

We followed the road along the northern edge of the Klaskino and found a place where we could easily load and launch in the morning. A layby on the other side of the road gave us just enough room to tuck the truck and our two tents. I was tired from the day's long drive, but as excited as a kid about tomorrow's departure.

At 5:55 AM I awoke to the ground literally shaking beneath me and a roaring sound that was louder than anything I'd ever heard. I was still dozy and lay somewhat stunned in my sleeping bag. The sound increased to a deafening level and then rode right over me. A powerful gust tried to obliterate my tent.

This was merely the first logging truck of the day.

I staggered out, my heart pounding. The thing must have passed within six feet of me. Shortly after, a pickup truck appeared and I flagged it down. I explained we were paddling to the Brooks for an extended period and asked if they had any suggestions as to the safest place to leave our vehicle. The two loggers were very friendly and told us they had a camp just down the road and we were welcome to leave the truck there.

We loaded the kayaks, and after Mike had returned from parking the truck, launched into winds that were already nudging gale-force levels. We crossed to the far side of the inlet and hugged the shore, managing to escape some of the wind's impact as we made our way towards Jims Creek. We pulled up to the creek mouth, hauled our kayaks above the high tide line, and then walked inland. The stream flowed gently around towering Sitka spruce, over naturally sculptured wood and stone, and into quiet, deep-green pools. Unfortunately, the whole area was in the process of being logged to within yards of the creek. Mike had been here the previous fall by himself, when the salmon were spawning and black bears were in abundance. The difference between then and now, in the amount of encroaching clearcut, was apparently substantial.

Saddened, we paddled on to the next creek marked on the chart. To the right stood a recently built shack, with a set of antlers nailed above the partially opened door. We approached and knocked. There seemed to be no one around, so we looked in. Like the grounds outside, it was a disgusting mess; beer bottles and garbage seemed to lie everywhere. There was a note tacked to a beam, dated one month earlier:

> "I broke my kayak paddle so stayed here for two days while I fashioned a new one. Many people come here because of the beautiful falls and if you cleaned up around your place and took your garbage away, others might also be inclined to respect the area. . . . "

We followed the creek and climbed up the steep gradient, finding a number of idyllic pools and waterfalls. We sat and basked in the tranquillity, took some photos, then filled our water bags.

We paddled on, managing to avoid the main onslaught of the wind, which Mike guessed now to be thirty-five knots or more. Eventually we arrived at the mouth of the inlet and landed on a tiny, low tide beach on Heater Point. We walked over to the exposed side and looked down to the Brooks. The wind was howling! And the sea looked large and rough. No convincing was needed to stay put.

We set to levelling a couple of tent sites, but the wind shifted, leaving them much too vulnerable. We moved a bit further back, into a narrow cleft, and managed to terrace two spots on the steep, pebbled incline. We unloaded the gear and food we needed, then walked the kayaks across an already filling channel and secured them safely for the night. The tide continued to rise and our portion of Heater Point became a tiny island, surrounded by flooding waters.

At regular intervals a powerful "woosh...woomp" could be heard. To Mike it sounded like the blowing of a large whale, and on his previous trip he'd named this place "point-that-sounds-like-whale." Some time ago he'd discovered a book by Franz Boas which translated many of the evocative names Native people had given to places on Vancouver Island. To me, a reef called "place-of-many-fish" obviously recalled not only some good memories, but passed on, through language, valuable information. "Smith Reef," on the other hand, was pretty much a dead piece of news.

We soon discovered the blowhole from which the sound emanated. The open ocean swell swept in, and then both water and air were compressed into a narrow, upward chamber, creating the "woosh...woomp." We sat, and from the safety of our position watched the powerful sea unleash itself on the rugged shore. The clouds shifted; shafts of brilliant sunlight burst forth and shone down upon the silver-flecked water.

We cooked up another superb Mexican meal, then hung the food bag well off the ground. We'd seen a great deal of bear sign about and had no desire to risk late-night interruptions. The forecast indicated winds were to diminish to twenty-five knots overnight.

We were up at 6:00 AM. It was a cool forty-six degrees. We filled up on a good breakfast of french toast and coffee, then were off. We poked our noses out around the point. The swell was large but the breeze was mild.

"Here we go!" I said, excitement in my voice.

The sun rose and was delightfully warm; large white clouds drifted by. There was no "cap over the Cape."

In a couple of hours we reached McDougal Island in the mouth of the Klaskish Inlet, then aimed for what we thought would be the entrance to Brooks Lagoon. We passed the rough, confused seas off Orchard Point, and a long sandy beach came into view. The incoming swell exploded continuously along the full length of the shore. To the right a rock bluff rose up; beside it lay a long sandspit. Although we couldn't see clearly from our position, the chart indicated there was a good-sized creek between the bluff and the spit. A large lagoon, hidden from view, apparently lay behind.

We sat well outside the break line and examined the situation closely. The trick, it seemed, was to get in through the surf without capsizing or being killed, then to make a hard left behind the bluff into the calm and protected waters of the creek. Simple enough, I suppose . . . at least in theory.

Mike started to move, then dug in faster. He was off. I sat and waited to see the outcome. Suddenly a steep swell swept under me, lifting the stern so high that my bow buried itself in the sea. The wall of water moved rapidly past and chased the unaware Mike. He was too far away for me to shout, and even if I had, the roar of crashing surf would have drowned my effort.

The swell grew larger. Mike's kayak vanished, and I was presented with the bizarre picture of a huge wall of water upon which perched a small, capped head. Then there was only the cap. All evidence of Mike vanished and the wall flung downward into a tortured mass of driving water.

With the swell gone the sea flattened. Out of the white froth I saw a small kayak appear, intact, right side up, and with Mike still in it! He turned left and disappeared behind the bluff.

I shifted my attention to the task at hand. A series of

moderate swells moved under me, then off I went, heart pounding. The gods smiled again. I, too, arrived inside the breaking surf, right side up, dry, and in one piece.

I paddled into the clear, deep waters of the creek, rounded the end of the spit, and entered another world. The roar of crashing surf was well muffled by the large sandspit; the effect of increasing winds was likewise nullified and hardly a ripple disturbed the lagoon's surface. Forested peaks rose up before me in primal splendour. We landed and found that recent rains had erased any sign of previous human prints in the sand; the fresh wolf tracks we saw only served to emphasize the untouched, wild beauty.

Eventually we opted to set up camp on the lagoon side of the spit. I positioned my tent so the door would face the morning sun. The wind had risen to thirty knots, but the barrier of sand allowed only a refreshing breeze to blow over us — most welcome on this very hot August day. I discovered more wolf tracks; Mike found an immaculate white eagle feather. It seemed our arrival was well blessed with good omens!

After supper the wind died, and we walked up the short incline to the exposed side of the spit and sat sipping Cointreau. A flaming red sun sank into the depths of the open ocean and set the sky on fire.

~~~~~

Next morning the sun lifted over the mountains and shone down on the lagoon and our tents. Mist lifted off the calm waters. A flock of ducks approached, carved a slow turn, then drifted into a gentle landing. Gulls cried out; four eagles sat nearby . . . and Mike found more *very* fresh wolf tracks.

We cooked up my favourite breakfast of pancakes, this time laced with fresh huckleberries we'd picked the day before. A heavy fog bank hung offshore, obliterating our view of "point-that-sounds-like-whale"; otherwise, it was a cloudless sky on a perfect day.

We spent the day wandering on foot and paddling the lagoon and creek. I found a fresh water source that could only have been fashioned by a Zen gardener — every rock, branch, and piece of moss was subtly placed, allowing the water to slip delicately over a miniature cliff into our containers. Later, we made our way through the forest onto the long sandy beach we'd first spied upon our arrival. The gulls hovered by the hundreds upon hundreds; their never ending cries pierced the continual roar of crashing surf. We found tiny Japanese medicine bottles; big Japanese saki and whisky bottles; a Russian radio and bottle – but no sign of glass floats. As always, several eagles sat on high limbs and looked down upon us.

In the days that followed we left our spit and paddled to the southwest, exploring what seemed to be an infinite number of beaches. The fog continually taunted us, threatening to obscure everything. Often, after softly covering us, it would back off a mile or two, a dense, impenetrable grey.

One day, about mid-morning, we sat outside the surf off a high sandy beach that hid a large creek. Mike suddenly pointed. "Look!" A mature eagle swooped down out of the fog, directly towards the ocean's surface. There was a splash, then an incoming swell blocked our view. Moments later the bird reappeared, desperately trying to gain height, clutching what appeared to be a salmon in its talons. As the eagle angled up over the high sandbank, the fish fell. The fog closed in. With the same thought in mind, we both sprinted for the beach, successfully dealing with the surf and landing next to the creek mouth. The fog thinned, creating a magical world of bright light, with wisps of swirling white. Mike headed off for the catch. Alas, all he found were glistening silver scales lying on the warm sand. The eagle had obviously regained its catch.

I found what appeared to be a new plastic clothes basket, about two feet in diameter. I cut off the bottom, kept the circular rim, then took some fishnet I'd found and fastened it with nylon twine. This left me with a six- to eight-inch-deep pouch with a plastic rim on top. Not classy, but probably effective enough to catch some crab. I lashed it to the rear deck of my kayak.

After lunch we walked well up the creek, then retraced our steps, and managed to successfully launch through the

incoming surf. The fog moved in and turned the world
ahead of us a light grey; then everything was erased from
sight. We stayed close to shore and each other; our eyes
and ears strained for warning signs. We paused near a bed
of kelp and I quickly caught a rockfish to use as bait in the
crab trap. An ethereal Merlin waved his magical wand and
the fog thinned, the mountains materialized, and the warm
sun smiled upon us.

Back at camp I gutted the fish and tied it tightly with
fishing line to the bottom of the pouch. I fastened some
rocks for weight and attached fifty feet of line, the other
end of which was connected to an orange float I'd found.
Shortly before tide change, I dropped the whole rig in deep
water not far from the creek mouth.

Half an hour later I paddled out and positioned myself
above the trap, took up the slack on the line, then pulled
as hard and fast as I could . . . the idea being that speed
and pressure would keep any critters in the pouch. "Wow!
I've got three huge Dungeness crabs," I shouted to Mike. I
returned one to the water and then lashed the net to my
deck and headed to shore.

"It may not be salmon, but it's still going to be a gour-
met seafood dinner tonight," I forecast. And so it was. A
9.5 on the "Lagoon Scale Of Dining Excellence."

Later, the fog reappeared and thickened. By the time I
went to bed, everything was truly socked in. I looked out
about 3:00 AM. No stars, and everything was very, very damp.

⌐᷼᷼᷼⌐

For the next few days the fog stayed with us. Still, we
managed to explore the beautiful Klaskish River and East
Creek estuaries. The fog started to thin and Mike made a solo
effort at reaching the Cape, but was turned back by rough
seas. Then the fog rolled in, thicker than ever. The forecast
indicated it would probably be with us for days to come. We
heated up some fresh water and indulged in a wonderful hot
shower and made plans to depart in the morning.

⌐᷼᷼᷼⌐

I looked out my tent at 5:30 AM; the sky was covered with dense, dark cloud. By breakfast, patches of blue could be seen; then the sun broke through on the mountains around us. We decided to postpone leaving. It was a restful day that followed. I slowly cleaned my kayak and made some minor repairs, washed clothes, caught up on my journal, and spent an endless amount of time watching a peregrine falcon hunt sandpipers.

The sun was profoundly healing . . . it was warm and soothing, dried my clothes, and made all right with the world. I could see why people worshipped the sun. I too became an ardent convert. In the afternoon I fell asleep on the warm sand, with the orchestra playing the muffled symphony of pounding surf in the background.

Just after midnight I was awakened by Mike calling out: "You've got to see this. The bio-luminescence is incredible." I put on some clothes and crawled out. Never had I seen it so concentrated. Even my footprints sparkled when I walked close to the receding tide line. Small flounders swam away at my approach, leaving bright luminous trails. A swish of my boot in the water stirred swirl upon swirl of vivid, flashing light. Above me, the night canopy was crystal-clear and filled with an infinite number of stars. I crawled back into my warm down bag, closed my eyes, and imagined wolves walking on the wild beaches we'd explored earlier.

At 6:00 AM, we listened to the VHF radio: "Northwest winds to twenty-seven knots and gusting." It would be an arduous paddle back to Klaskino Inlet. In addition, it was cold. Our breath hung in the air and Mike's thermometer indicated it was only forty-two degrees on this late-August morning. We packed our gear and launched. Paddling out of the lagoon, I experienced a sense of perverse joy when a swell unexpectedly broke across Mike's kayak and slammed him full in the chest. "Too bad!" I shouted, as I skilfully shot past him.

My joy was to be short-lived. We were paddling directly

into the prevailing wind and sea, and before long I, too, was soaked. The swells outside the lagoon were eight to ten feet high, many of them breaking. Mike guessed the wind to be coming in gusts of twenty-five to thirty knots. The first hour was not inspiring; I questioned whether we even made any significant movement. The shore still seemed awfully close. My kayak punched through the breaking crests and sometimes dropped with a horrendous crash. The sound was sickening. I prayed to the God of Fibreglass to keep my craft glued together.

Eventually the wind established a regular gusting pattern. It seemed to mellow for several minutes at a time, and I became aware that we were actually gaining ground. Mike continued to pull ahead, his paddle blades, the size of snow shovels, whirling away. Then a gust would hit and for the next minute or two it would be all I could do to hold my ground. The seas, although big and rough, were really quite manageable. It was the wind that slowly wore me down. Mike was soon a good hundred and fifty yards ahead. Now and then I could glimpse his toque. Finally he stopped and waited for me to catch up.

"What do you think?" he asked. "Should we turn back?"

"No. If you don't mind waiting for me, I'll be okay. I'm definitely doing well between the gusts."

We paddled on, and after another hour our progress became evident and most encouraging. I caught a second wind and the remaining distance became an easier challenge. Finally we rounded "point-that-sounds-like-whale." Despite wearing paddling jackets, we were soaked, inside and out, from sweat and sea. We landed and suddenly felt quite chilled. We moved behind a large rock, out of the wind, and let the sun beat down and warm our tired bodies. We refuelled our motors with peanut butter and jam sandwiches.

Only a seven-mile paddle down the inlet remained, and the wind would be nicely at our backs. The journey's end was in sight. Already we were talking about returning.

THE INCIDENT

THE INCIDENT

~~~~~

IT WAS A calm, sun-drenched morning as Mike and I paddled out through the Chain Islets off Victoria. So calm that nearby yachts sat motionless, their sails hanging limply. The forecast called for an approaching low, expected to bring gale-force winds by evening.

We soon reached Discovery Island and paddled along its southern shore. Today we saw no one. A pair of eagles perched in their usual tree; a mink scampered across the beach, oblivious to our presence; several dozen seals lay on low-lying rock. As we neared Seabird Point, I looked for Tom or Vera, the lighthouse keepers, but saw neither. We moved quickly, swept along by the last of the flood, and eventually pulled in at a favourite white shell beach on the island's north side.

It was after lunch that we noticed the first wind gusts.

They were from the south, and although we were well protected, the tops of the trees bent in telltale fashion. There
were no clouds, just clear blue sky. It seemed unlikely that
the predicted gale had arrived this early. Perhaps it was a
local phenomenon due to the unusual heat. We soon dis-
missed the idea as the gusts strengthened and then became
an increasingly steady blow. We began to ponder what the
sea conditions would be like on the return trip. Baynes Channel could be wicked with strong winds opposing the current.
There was some consolation in knowing that if worse came
to worse we could always impose upon the generosity of the
lighthouse keepers and spend the night with them.

We launched and paddled along the channel between
Discovery and Chatham islands. The force of the wind
soon became quite evident. The seas in the shallow waters
were mild, but the wind was now blowing a good thirty-five
to forty knots. Mike, with his powerful stroke, was able to
make some progress. I quickly realized that my ability to
gain any ground was absolutely minimal.

Mike turned and suggested we scoot across to the protected side of Chatham and see how things looked at the
northern tip, out across Baynes Channel. I thought it would
be even worse; still, we obviously weren't going anywhere
very fast here. It was also evident that the islands afforded
enough protection from the powerful southern winds to
allow us safe return to Discovery and the lighthouse if necessary. We paddled past picnickers on the protected sand
beach on Chatham, their open aluminum and fibreglass
runabouts resting on the shore. I wondered how they
would get back to Victoria!

We ran our kayaks up onto the beach in Puget Cove
and portaged across the short distance to the west side of
the island. It was only then that we saw the true ferocity of
the storm. Out in Baynes Channel the winds, which we later
learned were gusting to sixty knots, clashed headlong with
the increasing ebb, creating steep, nine-foot breaking seas.

We slid our kayaks into waters superbly protected by
Vantreight and the most western Chatham Island. There were

at least ten craft huddled here, including a beautiful old launch, several large sailboats, and a vulnerable looking speedboat. We paddled easily amongst them, over to the furthest islet, got out, and walked to the exposed side. The wind was screaming.

We watched a large sailboat attempt to motor through the north end of Baynes Channel. It would rise up on a steep wave, plunge downward, and, not having enough time to rise again, be smothered by the next breaking sea. Then, shuddering, it would rise up, and the bow would break free, only to be slammed by the wind. Through our binoculars we could see the craft literally twisted and blown sideways. Eventually it turned and ran for the more protected waters behind Ten Mile Point. I swung my gaze to the south and saw a ship, perhaps 250 feet in length, approaching. It was the *J.P. Tully*, a federal vessel. The rough seas seemed to have little impact on its progress, although I noticed that when turned broadside to the raging wind even it heeled over. It moved slowly past, eventually halting north of the channel entrance.

We walked back to the lee of the little island and discussed plans. Although we always carried extensive emergency gear, even on day outings, it seemed a lot cosier to make our way back to Tom and Vera at the lighthouse than to set up camp. I'd also be able to call my wife and let her know not to worry should we have to spend the night.

We paddled lazily along the protected side of Vantreight Island, and then noticed the Auxiliary Coast Guard vessel, the *Responder*, coming in from the appalling conditions in Baynes Channel. A tow rope stretched out behind, and we saw a portion of an overturned hull in the water. We paddled closer. There was much discussion by the crew as to what to do with the capsized craft (apparently a fishing boat about forty feet in length). One of them called out to us and asked if we could assist in running a line to shore, thus securing the sunken boat. I paddled over, got the line, and took it to Mike, who had now landed on the beach. He wrapped it tightly around the base of a large tree. Meanwhile,

the *Responder* had moved close enough to allow one of the
crew to leap out and assist Mike. They got to talking. Apparently, the fishing boat had capsized in the heavy seas,
and the *Responder* had managed to rescue the two fishermen,
now cold but no worse for wear, and tow the overturned
craft into these safer waters.

It was then that the crewman asked Mike if we wanted
a ride back to Victoria with them. Mike hesitated. "Well,
we've got our kayaks."

"No problem, we've taken kayaks before. We'll just
throw them on either side of the deck."

We didn't reply. But what a tempting offer! It was becoming increasingly obvious that we wouldn't be able to
paddle home tonight. The option of being safe in Victoria
in twenty minutes was *most* appealing. The twenty-five-foot
Responder moved back and forth in the protected waters. A
smaller speedboat, the *Scorpion*, with two other members
from the Auxiliary Coast Guard, pulled alongside them.
Much talk ensued. Then one of them shouted out, "Want a
ride or not?" I hesitated. Mike yelled back, "Sure."

And so it came about that we climbed aboard, hauling
up our kayaks on either side of the *Responder*'s deck. Wow!
A ride on an Auxiliary Coast Guard vessel ... home in
twenty minutes!

But we didn't head back. Instead we continued to motor
about in the bay. There was discussion about a small sailboat
in possible danger as it dragged its anchor and came closer to
the shore. The *Responder* edged over and ran its nose onto
the beach. Two of the crew leapt out and talked with the
owner of the craft while Mike and I used a long pole to
keep the stern of the *Responder* perpendicular to the beach.
We got increasingly wet as the swell broke against the
stern. The wind added a further chilling dimension.

It was at this point that I began expressing my doubts
to Mike. "Isn't this the same rescue boat that got swept
onto the rocks last year trying to help someone?" He nodded affirmatively. "Well, I sure as hell hope they've got a
different crew on today," I muttered. I decided it would be

wise to put on some warmer clothing. Both Mike and I were wearing polypropylene long underwear under nylon pants and wool shirts, in addition to our paddling jackets and life vests. I opened my rear kayak hatch and pulled out some extra gear. I found a heavy poly top, my lovely wool toque, and a pair of neoprene gloves I'd only recently purchased and never before worn. I secured the rear hatch and left the gear bags in the open cockpit.

Eventually we pulled off the beach, turned, and again came alongside the *Scorpion* for further discussion between the two crew. We overheard talk about a woman and her baby on one of the sailboats wanting a ride back. We motored over. One of the crew shouted, "Throw them on." The others talked further, and wisely concluded that we already had more than enough people on board.

Still we did not head out, but continued to motor back and forth in the waters behind Vantreight Island. Further doubts crept into my mind. I remembered by friend Philip's words, when he'd talked of rescuing people: "Never take a person from a place of safety into a place of danger." It made sense. Were we being stupid in not choosing to stay on Discovery? Again I hesitated, and said nothing.

Finally the *Responder* turned, the engine roared, and we headed out — but still not back to Victoria! Instead we ventured northwest, out into the entrance of Baynes Channel. Two sailboats were visible, neither in apparent distress. Beyond them lay the large *J.P. Tully*. It was terribly rough. In less than a minute Mike and I were drenched; my yellow Helly Hanson yacht boots filled. Water poured over the bow and cabin as we pounded into the raging seas. Mike and I sat with the fishermen, huddled in the false protection of the cabin on the open deck. The *Responder* turned and motored back into protected waters.

By now I was decidedly unimpressed with what was happening. Then, less than a minute later, we headed back into open waters, towards Jemmy Jones Island. "Why are we going this route?" I shouted. Mike raised his eyebrows and held on tightly to the boat as we slammed into the first big seas. In kayaks, we practically always crossed the channel further south, as the standing waves and turbulent water were known to be wicked in this portion. "Ah well," I thought, "I guess it doesn't make that big a difference when you're in something this powerful."

The *Responder* would plough into a steep sea, rise up, then plummet into the trough, which was too narrow to allow us to rise up again. The next wave would roar across the deck, drenching us. We all held on for dear life. We were miserably cold. "Thank God this'll all soon be over and we'll be safe on dry land," I thought. One of the crew, Paul, stood at the stern on the open deck, facing us, tightly clutching a large stanchion. He was dressed from head to toe in a bright yellow all-weather suit. He stood firmly, feet well planted. He smiled and seemed to be enjoying the ride.

Almost level with Jemmy Jones Island, the *Responder* slowed and turned northwards. "What's going on?" I shouted to Mike. We crashed downwards again. My kayak started to float and water swirled around my feet, rising to my waist.

My awareness slowed to a crawl. I was now waist deep in water . . . now my feet seemed to be losing touch with the deck. My mind wound in slow motion trying to absorb the impossible fact that the *rescue* boat was sinking!

"Don't worry," Paul shouted out, trying to keep everyone calm. "This boat will *not* sink. It will *not* sink." A moment of bizarre humour entered my thoughts. "Sure, sure, it won't sink. This guy's taken lessons on the *Titanic!*" Then another thought shot swiftly through: "If the rescue boat sinks in this sort of weather, then who comes to rescue us?"

The boat moved out from under me; my kayak drifted off. For whatever reason, I dove for it. Technically, Paul was right. The *Responder* did not sink. The motor died, the boat filled with water, and with a slight shudder it settled into the sea and capsized. The overturned white hull was low in the water and virtually invisible in the foam and froth of the wild seas and screaming wind.

I know you're supposed to stay with the boat, but I'd lost all faith in the *Responder*. Besides, there was this irrational feeling of not wanting to lose my beloved kayak. I watched helplessly as my cockpit filled with a breaking sea and instantly all my gear bags and a $265 paddle were swept away. I knew that despite the water in the cockpit, the fore and aft hatches were firmly closed and watertight — she would float.

The water was bitterly cold this spring day. I grabbed the stern of the kayak; another sea slammed into my face and I let go. I recovered and swam two quick strokes and grabbed the hull again. It was then that I noticed a smiling, bobbing face encased in bright yellow holding onto the bow of my kayak. It was Paul. How nice to have company! One of the fishermen surfaced beside me. He looked absolutely frigid. He turned and started to try to swim for Jemmy Jones Island. One of the crew shouted to him and succeeded in calling him back.

It was then that I heard other crew members crying out, "Fred! Fred!" We had apparently all surfaced with the exception of Fred, a retired naval captain in his mid-sixties, who'd been in the *Responder*'s cabin. There was a desperate tone in the men's voices as they tried to be heard over the howl of wind and sea. It appeared that Fred had either surfaced far from us, or had been trapped underneath the hull.

Paul and I drifted away from the capsized craft. Jemmy Jones Island was temptingly close. For a moment I, too, toyed with the notion of trying to swim for it. It was then that I recognized the illusion of being swept by the waves towards the rocky islet. In fact, the current was actually taking us out into the centre of Baynes Channel and away from Jemmy Jones. Paul and I held onto the kayak and tried kicking our way back to the wallowing *Responder*. After some moments we realized there was no hope in that effort.

I had a last glance at the capsized boat as I rode up on a particularly high wave. The barely visible hull seemed to be awash in violent seas. I could see several heads above the water, and the men appeared to be trying to haul themselves up onto the overturned craft. I was again blasted off the kayak by a wall of water, but managed to hang on to one of the rudder cables and then pull myself partially out of the water again by lying over the hull. The neoprene gloves were turning out to be a true lifesaver. Without them, I would already have lost any meaningful dexterity and strength in the freezing water and chilling wind.

I was now thoroughly cold and my teeth were chattering. Things looked exceedingly grim. Five men were clinging to an overturned boat, the sixth had apparently drowned, and two of us were drifting into the roughest part of the channel in the worst winds in thirty-five years. As far as I knew, there was no hope for rescue. I assumed that no one was even aware that we had gone down.

At the other end of my kayak, Paul looked intense but comfortable. He shouted out encouraging words. "We're going to make it. Hang on. I'm sure they got off a MAYDAY." My spirits were buoyed by his presence and his words, but I had far less faith than he that a MAYDAY had been sent. (I was wrong. Apparently they *had* got a signal off.) As we drifted, I was knocked from the stern of the kayak with great regularity by the raging seas, but each time managed to pull myself half up and over the hull again.

Paul and I talked about whether there was a chance of swimming back to either the *Responder* or over to Jemmy Jones, but common sense prevailed and we stayed with the drifting kayak. "They'll get us!" Paul shouted. "We're good for a long time yet." It was then that it struck me how different our respective positions were. Paul was fully encased in his wonderful head-to-toe suit and probably *was* good for a considerable time to come, while I had on only minimal gear for ocean swimming in these frigid waters. Prior to the *Responder* sinking, I'd already been thoroughly soaked and chilled for a substantial period of time.

"You may be good for few hours," I yelled to Paul, "but I don't know how much longer I can hang on."

Paul spoke intently. "We're going to make it, you hear! We're going to make it! They'll get us." His words helped.

I told Paul I had a flare-gun tucked in the cockpit, which I thought he might reach from his position on the bow. "We'll be okay," he said.

"I think we should fire it," I replied.

Paul reached in and quickly found the flare-gun in its zip-lock wrapping. Unfortunately, neither of us had sufficient dexterity left to undo the wretched bag! Eventually we each placed a corner of the "zip" in our mouths and pulled, opening it. To our horror we found I'd double-bagged it! I tried shedding the second bag with my teeth, but they were chattering too much, and I no longer had sufficient strength to fully clamp down. Paul tried several times and then succeeded. He broke the gun open and very slowly, talking himself along, loaded the first shell. "Now, let's see . . . first we break the barrel open . . . put the shell in here . . . snap it shut. . . . " I cocked the hammer and Paul took it, aiming well into the howling wind. We shot one flare, then repeated the whole procedure and fired a second into the sky.

It was then that I noticed the *J.P. Tully* still hovering well off the north end of the channel. To my unbelieving eyes it looked as though they had just lowered one of their launches.

Yes! Yes! They had. And it was now actually pounding its way through the rough seas towards the *Responder*. I told Paul to fire a third flare if he could. I felt we were so low in the water and the conditions so rough and confused that the *Tully*'s launch would pass us by. Paul managed a third flare and I saw the launch, aptly named the *Tempest*, turn towards us.

It was then that I knew for sure that we were going to make it.

The *Tempest* came alongside — what a glorious sight! It tossed and turned, but seemed a remarkably sturdy craft. A crewman threw us a line, which missed completely, but the helmsman then turned and was able to drag it closer. Hanging on to the kayak, we kicked and swam towards it. We grabbed it! They pulled hard. I no longer had the strength to haul myself up out of the water. Two men reached over and lifted me onto the deck, then Paul, and, joy of joys, they flung my kayak aboard as well.

One of the men pushed me down into the cabin and

told me to wrap up in blankets. I pulled off some of my wet clothes; my teeth chattered, my whole body shivered nonstop. I meticulously stored the wet garments and my life-jacket in the cockpit, not wanting any of it to be lost. I wrapped myself in a blanket and then turned to look outside. Paul appeared to be in good shape, standing on the aft deck in his brilliant yellow, talking with the *Tempest*'s two crew.

Eventually I saw the overturned hull of the *Responder* and I shouted out, "There's the other boat, there's the *Responder*." One of the *Tempest*'s crew shouted back, "It's okay, it's okay. They've all been picked up by other boats."

We altered course and headed for shore.

~~~~~~

When all was said and done, it turned out that all of us on the *Responder* were rescued, escaping death and serious injury. Fred, the retired naval captain, was apparently trapped for some twelve minutes in the overturned hull, in an air pocket, before making good his escape. The *Responder* was found several days later, drifting off Friday Harbour in the American San Juan Islands. Miraculously, Mike's kayak was found floating and intact, trapped underneath.

The whole event was best summed up by my four-year-old daughter when a friend said how fortunate we were not to have died. She replied: "It wasn't Daddy's time yet."

CLOSE . . . VERY CLOSE

CLOSE . . . VERY CLOSE

THE BRIGHT, MID-JUNE sun bounced off the ocean's flat surface, directly into my unprotected eyes. I put the paddle down, pulled on sunglasses, and tugged the brim of my hat lower. In the distance, the majestic mountains of the Olympic Peninsula rose up out of a low-level mist which covered the far side of Juan de Fuca Strait.

Mike, Ed, and I had launched off Victoria's Oak Bay and headed over to Discovery Island for a pleasant day's paddle. We meandered through the Chain Islets, which were full of nesting gulls and cormorants. Two eagles flew low overhead, creating screaming chaos amongst the birds, while hundreds of seals continued to bask on the rocks, undisturbed by the commotion. It was one of those calm, uneventful days, with no frightening extremes of current or wind that could so quickly turn this wonderland into a mess of powerful, rough seas.

We stopped on the north side of Discovery and wandered through the idyllic meadows and forest, then paddled on, past the lighthouse at Seabird Point. We pulled in at Rudlin Bay and sat on the beach, contentedly eating lunch. We were completely sheltered from any breeze and it was unbelievably hot for this time of year. I stretched out on the warm pebbles and contemplated a brief nap. As my eyelids gently closed, I glimpsed a huge dorsal fin slowly sliding under the water. I bolted upright. "My God! I think I just saw . . . "

" . . . a whale!" Mike completed my sentence. "I thought I saw it, too."

All three of us stood upright. Yes! There it was . . . a large male orca, and now a cow and a calf rising beside it. Wow! This was Ed's first time paddling in these waters and so I nonchalantly lied, "It happens all the time out here, Ed."

I ran and got my binoculars and looked out, about one hundred yards from shore. "I see another six ahead of them," I said. They moved slowly, on a course that would take them over to Trial Island, then down the Strait of Juan de Fuca towards Race Rocks and the open west coast. We talked excitedly about our good fortune in seeing the killer whales, then packed our gear and leisurely paddled out.

CRAAACK! Our heads snapped around, just in time to see three more whales round the point, one of whom was slamming its flukes on the water with dramatic force.

"Look, there's more behind them," shouted Mike. Later, we estimated thirty-five orca passed, travelling in groups of two and three.

Ed and I paddled over to the edge of a large kelp bed off Rudlin Bay, while Mike moved further on, to the shallow waters adjacent to Commodore Point. The whales passed by, about a city block in front of us. One rose up, "spy hopping" — standing vertically in the water and looking about. Behind us we heard even louder crashes and looked to see one flinging herself out of the water and landing on her side, sending volumes of water into the air.

They seemed big, especially the males with their huge

dorsal fins. There also seemed to be a surprising number of calves in the pod. We stayed tucked beside the kelp bed, well to the side of their route, having no desire to upset any caring mother.

"Oh-oh!" shouted Ed. "I think we've just become part of the flight path."

I turned and looked. A giant male, cow, and calf had broken from the rest of the group and were now aimed directly at us. Ed and I stayed put while Mike backed further into the shallow waters of the reef. The rest of the pod continued by, their high-pitched squeals clearly audible. I tapped, drum-like, on the deck of my kayak. "Just in case they don't know we're here," I said nervously to Ed.

"WHOOSH!" —just off to my right, between us and the shore, rose the family of three. So big, so sleek, so close! It was amazing. They passed very close to Mike, which was even more astounding, given how shallow the water under him.

"Behind you!" shouted Ed. I whipped my head around. Literally a foot or so from my stern a dorsal fin cut the surface. The displaced water nudged my kayak gently forward. Another came at me from the left, then calmly rolled on its side and passed directly beneath me. I stared at the large mouth and single eye; the brilliant white patches seemed close enough to touch.

The beautiful beast slipped away, effortlessly, and was gone.

It was an unbelievable moment.

I sat and watched the pod move on. A smile covered my face from ear to ear.

Next day I was out paddling by myself. I came across my friend Philip, sitting alone on the shore of Chatham Island, his small sailing craft tucked in a nearby bay. I told him of yesterday's experience. He nodded and smiled in a knowing fashion.

"Awhile back I was sailing down Haro Strait," he said. "I'd just put on a tape of Paul Horn playing his flute when suddenly I was surrounded by porpoises. They stayed with me until the tape ended, then were gone."

"It's quite amazing," I replied, "especially when you consider they choose to seek us out . . . it seems they have a wonderfully benign curiosity about us. If you think about it, that was a very vulnerable moment when the one whale passed right underneath me. One flick of a tail, one bite, and I'd have been nothing more than a collage of bone bits and fibreglass!"

Philip chuckled. "Yes, they don't seem as malicious towards our species as we've been to theirs. I've always felt they were far more evolved."

I nodded in agreement.

A GRAND JOURNEY

A GRAND JOURNEY

THROUGHOUT THE WINTER, Mike and I pored over maps of Vancouver Island's west coast. Eventually we concocted a tentative plan to paddle from north of the Brooks Peninsula down to the Tofino area, almost half the length of the west coast of the island. Overall, I had mixed feelings about the project. On the one hand, I was excited about the adventure of it; on the other, I was scared stiff! Reading a variety of sailing guides about the region only served to rattle my confidence and make me question the sanity of our scheme. The more I thought about kayaking this forbidding stretch of coastline, the higher my level of anxiety rose. Eventually it became quite evident to me that there were at least three spots I could count on dying: rounding Cape Cook, passing Bajo Reef off Nootka Island, and getting through the rock and reef minefield surrounding Estevan Point.

Despite all the doubts and fear, I couldn't bring myself to back out. The plan offered the potential for a wonderful adventure that would take us through territory renowned for its wild, rugged beauty. It would be a true challenge, not only in kayaking and outdoor skills, but even more so in just dealing with myself. In the end I gave up analyzing it all. My heart said, "Go," and I went with that.

~~~~~

And so it came to pass that at 6:30 AM on a Saturday late in August, we found ourselves on the seaplane dock in Tofino. Our pilot, Terry, was an amiable sort. He skilfully lashed our kayaks to the single-engine Beaver, one kayak tied over each pontoon. Our gear was loaded inside and then we taxied out into the smooth but fast-flowing ebb. There was an increasing roar as we pushed along, then broke free of the water's grasp and were airborne. Terry pulled the aircraft up steeply, dropped a wing, and carved a tight turn northwards.

The flight itself was a gem of an experience. Terry flew at about 110 MPH at a low altitude, over the exact route we intended to paddle. Huge cloud formations lay all around, but good fortune and the pilot's skills allowed us a clear view all the way up the coast. We stared in awe at what lay below. The predominant theme seemed to be inaccessible shoreline bordered by dark, menacing rock, awash in the swirling white of exploding seas. At one point I saw Bajo Reef clearly etched below. It looked like an ugly place to die!

"What's the weather supposed to be like up on the Brooks?" I shouted to Terry over the engine noise.

"Don't know," he replied. "We'll see when we get there. Exactly where do you guys want to land?"

"Well, somewhere in the Klaskish Inlet would be great, but it may be too windy. If we can't land there, it'll have to be either Klaskino Inlet or Quatsino Sound."

Terry proceeded to pull out and examine an old, well-worn Texaco road map. I paled and turned to Mike, who quickly found one of our far more detailed charts and passed it forward.

In about an hour and a quarter we reached the northern shore of the wild Brooks Peninsula. Terry had kindly flown right out to the tip of the Brooks, then cut between the Cape and Solander Island. We were low enough to easily see the large Stellar sea lions basking on the rocks below. The sun cast its morning light on waters that had lain in the shadow of the mountains. Barely a ripple disturbed the surface. We could not have asked for a better day.

"You two *are* in luck," said Terry. "I could put her down over there if you want." He pointed to a cove on the southern shore of the Klaskish Inlet.

"That would be great," Mike replied.

Terry dropped the Beaver down, and with fine skill, softly ushered us into shallow waters about twenty yards from shore.

"I left some other guys here once. They paddled down to Hot Springs and flew out from there. *If* you make it that far, we fly in there all the time; it's only a few minutes by air to Tofino. Be glad to give you a lift."

I noted the "If you make it," but let it pass and thanked him kindly for his offer.

I leapt into the thigh-deep water, in shorts and running shoes, and unlashed the kayaks. Mike and Terry loaded the gear into the open cockpits and I was able to ferry it all to shore. In short order we were done. We said our goodbyes to Terry and thanked him profusely for the wonderful flight.

With a roar the plane moved out and lifted off. He rose quickly, circled, then flew over us, dipping the wings in farewell. Then he was gone from sight. All was quiet, except for the muffled sound of endless incoming surf. We stood alone, on the very spot we'd been the previous year. Time seemed to shift. It was easy to imagine we'd never left.

We took ages to load. As always, my smaller kayak never seemed to have enough room, and we embarked upon the inevitable discussion about whether I should finally give serious consideration to buying a larger-volume craft. As usual, we got it all in, Mike with a disproportionate amount, both in quantity and weight. Then we were off, and soon out of the inlet's protection, into the powerful open sea. I felt good and very alive . . . a lot of life's complexities seemed to slip away.

We headed for the Brooks Lagoon, and it was not long before we rounded Orchard Point and I saw the familiar long, sandy beach. The swell roared in . . . endless sweeping rows that climbed, curled, and crashed upon the shore. We saw what appeared to be a salmon jump. I cast, and to my surprise, pulled in a small mackerel.

"Maybe it's the warming influence of the El Niño current," Mike said. "Keep your eyes open for great white sharks!" Then he was off, making a run for the protected waters of the lagoon. He manoeuvred his way through the surf, then turned hard left and disappeared behind the rocky bluff. I followed, and nearly capsized. A swell rose up, grabbed my stern, and threatened to fling me broadside, then upside down. A quick brace, and incredibly good fortune, saved me. I guess the gods thought it would be just too humiliating a way to start the *great journey*. The experience, however, had a most humbling effect, and made me pay much more attention thereafter.

We set up camp on the sandy spit, under hot, sunny skies. Scattered elsewhere were isolated, dark rain clouds. The sound of thunder echoed off the mountains. We put a tarp over the kitchen, on the off chance one of the heavy clouds might drift our way.

We opened the wine to celebrate our wonderful start, and cooked up a superb omelette dinner of free-range eggs, garlic, onions, shiitake mushrooms, cheese, and tomatoes, plus the ever-present hot sauce. A thunder shower let go over us and washed the world clean. The sun set in a blaze of brilliant orange.

All in all, it seemed a grand beginning.

～～～

I awoke at 5:00 AM and could hear Mike already moving about in his tent. Although neither of us had put words to our feelings, we were both quite anxious. Today we would probably reach and round the notorious Cape of

Storms. The sky was clear, the wind slept, and the sun lay hidden behind the forested mountains. A light mist covered the lagoon. We ate a quick breakfast, packed and moved out. Mike made it through the surf unscathed; I got clobbered by a breaking swell, which brought laughter and a smile from Mike.

The sun cleared the mountaintops and its warmth soon settled onto our backs. My wet clothing dried quickly. The fog stayed well out to sea and the wind continued to sleep. We paddled along shores we'd explored in great detail the previous year, then passed the last familiar landmark. The sandy beaches ended and wild, rock-strewn coves and rugged cliffs took their place. Landing looked virtually impossible, even on a day as benign as this.

We wove through dangerous reefs and avoided the explosive, dumping seas that washed over barely submerged rock. A short distance from the cape we spied a beautiful waterfall, plummeting from a great height down the side of a cliff. We surveyed the area closely but saw nowhere to land. Reluctantly we paddled on. A few minutes later we spied a small cove protected by wicked-looking rocks. The swell broke every which way, creating rough and confused seas.

"What do you think?" Mike shouted.

"Sure, let's have a try . . . by the way, you going first?"

Mike nodded, moved forward, and skilfully showed the way through the narrow entrance. I waited, heart rate definitely at an elevated beat, then successfully made my way in behind him. It was a lovely little beach, complete with its own stream and hidden waterfall. We sat, munched a couple of granola bars, and debated whether to set up camp. It was now 11:00 AM, normally a time when the daily winds would begin to mount and thoughts turned to getting off the water. Yet this morning, hardly a breath of wind was in the air. There was unspoken agreement that we'd both feel much better once around the Cape.

We launched and picked our way through the dicey opening and made our way on. Little "cat's paws" blew across the water — that was it for wind.

Twenty minutes later we were there, sitting off the Cape of Storms! The swell was gentle, about six feet high and well spaced; the wind blew all of two knots. (A commercial fisherman later said to me, "Ah yes, you do get one or two days a year like that off the Cape!")

About a mile to the southwest lay Solander Island. It rose straight up some three hundred feet in all its rugged beauty. Incoming swells exploded on the bare rock of the exposed side; on the other, brilliant green foliage clung to the protected cliff. The sky was filled with sea birds, and to Mike's delight, many of them were his favourite — tufted puffins. A large colony of Stellar sea lions barked and roared. Two of them suddenly broke the surface next to us, then plunged below.

It was a moment to savour.

Eventually we moved off, leaving the little jewel behind. The wind and current increased — both against us. Paddling the fully loaded kayaks was tiring. In the excitement of it all, we'd neglected our regular breaks for water, and I suspect had become somewhat dehydrated on this sweltering day. Still, we slowly made ground. There were some surprises, as seas suddenly rose up indicating shallow rock and hidden reef. All in all, however, it was a most gentle day. Mike threaded a course through the obstacles and we eventually found ourselves sitting off a cove that seemed to beckon us ashore. No further urging was needed. After surveying the scene, we shifted course slightly, avoiding nasty rocks and dumping swells, and landed easily on the sandy beach, in the mildest of surf.

Ashore there were bear tracks everywhere, and wolf as well. We set up camp, then wandered over to the far end of the beach. We found a rushing creek, with a natural dam that had created some lovely deep pools. I stripped and stepped in. Arrgh! Once out, however, it was wonderful to stand in the warm sun, tingling all over.

We had an early dinner, topped off with a couple of chilled beer I'd secretly brought along to toast our success in rounding the Cape. We raised our drinks and thanked the Guardian Spirits for their kind and benevolent manner.

We were up at 6:00 AM and had a sumptuous breakfast of blueberry pancakes and hot coffee. Again the sky was unmarked by cloud — not even a hint of wind. We packed and were soon off, staying well clear of the dangerous shoals, and eventually entered territory we'd explored in previous years. At Clerke Point we moved in closer to shore and paddled at a relaxed, steady pace. I set up my fishing rod and trolled. The line suddenly screamed out and my thoughts ran wild with fantasies of the ever-elusive salmon. After much effort I pulled the fish close enough to catch a glimpse of a very, very large lingcod. I had no desire to have it in the boat with me; it was also overkill, as far as a meal for two was concerned. Eventually I was able to snug it alongside, grab the lure, and free the hook. The ling splashed violently, then dove for freedom.

We paddled on, stopped for lunch and another fresh-water bath in a deep-pooled creek, then crossed Nasparti Inlet, angling out to the O'Leary Islets — majestic rocks that jutted out of the open sea. Myriad sea birds hovered above, and large Stellar sea lions lay basking in the hot sun. One lone giant raised his head and let loose with a true jungle-lion roar. Mike answered with the best imitation he could muster. To our surprise and horror the mammoth creature turned and flung himself off the high ledge into the pounding sea below. None of the others moved so much as a single muscle. The lion's head broke the surface and he let go with another roar, then dove — straight for us.

"My God!" I shouted to Mike. "You've just imitated the mating cry of the passionately-in-heat female. You're in big trouble if this guy decides to mate with your kayak!"

We paddled like mad and did not see our friend again. The afternoon winds picked up and we soon found ourselves in mountainous seas that swept over the extensive area of reef off the outer side of the Cuttle Islets. My adrenaline kicked in and my eyes scanned the water ahead. Now and then one of the swells would rear up and dump in thunderous fashion on hidden rock. "Not a place to be!" I shouted above the roar, and pointed to where one particularly dramatic swell had just let go only a short distance to our right. Again Mike forged a safe route through the dangerous waters and we pulled into the safety of a tiny cove on one of the islets.

~~~~~

To our great delight the weather held and we continued our winding course along the coast. We moved from the Acous Peninsula over to the Bunsby Islands, then down to Thomas Island, where we paused midway in the crossing to Kyuquot. Mike sat ahead of me, his kayak gently rising and falling on the ever-present swell. To his right, a mature eagle perched high on a rocky outcrop and looked down with what I perceived to be a benevolent gaze. Over the years I'd come to regard their presence as a good omen. To date I hadn't been disappointed.

We moved on. I found the trip to be establishing a comfortable rhythm of its own. All stiffness seemed gone from my body, and as long as I maintained a healthy fluid intake, my endurance was easily up to par. Tasks such as establishing camp and cooking meals had become pleasant routine. All of these factors allowed my attention to shift more and more to the things around me.

Several days later we found ourselves passing magical Thornton Island late in the afternoon.

"What about stopping here for the night?" I suggested.

"We could, but we've always wanted to spend a night on Grassy, and it looks as though the weather will hold another day," replied Mike.

Grassy was a wonderful little island south of Kyuquot Sound. It was a rugged piece of rock, filled with fossils and covered in clinging bushes and wildflowers. There was a shell beach on the southern side where we'd often thought of camping. It was *not*, however, a place to be caught in a southerly storm.

"Sounds good. Let's go," I agreed.

We paddled on. Looking back over his right shoulder, Mike suddenly spied three kayakers who had apparently left the shores of Thornton and were now taking dead aim for *our* Grassy Island. We pushed hard, and it soon became obvious that an undeclared race was in progress. Paddles whirled like windmills in a storm.

"We're going to beat them!" I shouted.

We raced down the front of mild swells, rounded a rocky finger, and turned into the brilliant white beach. My smile vanished. There were already three tents, two people, and a couple of kayaks on the shore! A minute later the other three rounded the corner and landed behind us. In all my years of paddling, it was one of the few times we'd pulled into an intended campsite only to find someone else.

It was now late in the day and the thought of moving on, especially after the "race," was not an uplifting one. We elected to stay. It turned out that Mike and two of the other fellows had friends in common, so we spent a pleasant evening talking of past adventures. Later, dark clouds moved in and the radio warned of rain showers and an approaching low.

I was awakened in the middle of the night by the sound of rain beating down on my tent fly. I crawled deeper into my sleeping bag and tried to ignore it. In the morning it was obvious that our lengthy spell of good weather had taken a turn for the worse. We talked of staying, of paddling over to Kapoose Creek and waiting out the storm, or of moving on. Then a window opened. The rain stopped, the sun came out, and we decided to have breakfast and move down to Esperanza Inlet.

While we ate, the group of five packed and launched. Shortly after dismantling our gear and loading, the window closed. The clouds moved in and the temperature became markedly cooler. Mike paddled strongly and soon overtook the group. I lagged well behind, for I'd become quite chilled and had stopped to put on a heavier top and my paddling jacket. The wind was against us and water constantly blew off the paddle blade into my face; an occasional wave rolled across the deck and slapped me in the chest. I was warm and dry, and glad I'd taken the time to put the jacket on.

The five pulled into Tatchu Creek at Jurassic Point, apparently to collect water. We continued, then paused to check the route ahead. A disgusting reef extended a half-mile or more out to sea. To paddle out and around it, we first had to cross a shallow, rock-strewn bar. Mike waited, then made his move. He crossed the hazardous area safely, then was hit head on by the full force of a breaking swell. I didn't laugh. It was a dangerous spot, and a capsize would result in being ground into tiny little pieces on the sharp-edged, barnacled rock.

I sat, then sprinted forward. I, too, crossed safely, but, like Mike, was clobbered by the full force of the next swell. Fortunately, I managed to maintain my forward momentum, but water found its way past the tight cuffs of my jacket. Despite the advertiser's claim of the "ultimate in dryness," icy water poured down my sleeves and over my chest and stomach. Oh! So cold!

Once safely through, we clearly saw just how nasty the reef off Tatchu Point was. We angled out and gave ourselves ample room to clear the area. Now and then swells suddenly reared and crashed down with a vengeance. It was a tense time, but everything seemed relatively under control. As we rounded the reef we expected to find miserable conditions, what with an ebbing current meeting a southerly wind. Instead, it was surprisingly calm, and the further we moved into Esperanza Inlet, the calmer and calmer it became. I was soaked, but warm. The rain increased to a steady deluge.

The swells were now at our backs, which was most pleasant, and we had fun paddling down their gentle faces with little fear of capsize. Suddenly my rudder struck an unseen object, then, horror of horrors, I felt something graze the hull directly beneath me. Adrenaline raced through my body! I looked frantically into the depths but could see no sign of uncharted rock or reef. I felt the rudder hit again, and then heard a grinding sound, like teeth on metal! I was lost for an explanation.

My right hand pulled down and back on the paddle. A fin cut the water only inches from my wrist! Then another brushed alongside the cockpit. Mudsharks! Or more correctly, dogfish. That was what had been hitting the kayak. Maybe the vibration, or the sight, of the aluminum rudder had attracted or annoyed them? Now I could see them below. The water was thick with them. Some looked exceedingly long — four feet or more of shark. I felt much more relaxed now that I had an explanation for the bumps and grinding. It was also nice to know that these creatures were not known to do nasty things to man. Mind you, I had no intention of capsizing to test the theory out.

Mike was now well ahead of me, aiming for a nice-looking shore, backed by a large cliff, on Catala Island. The rain intensified and beat down on the calm water with a deafening roar. The beach was a steep one, covered in round stones, which created their own unique sound as they continually rolled in and out with the momentum of the swell. By the time I safely landed, Mike was already checking the area for a good site. I climbed up the shore and saw a large cave mouth in the cliff wall.

"This looks like a good spot to be if the rains are going to continue," said Mike. "If we put the tents right up against the cliff, we'll probably avoid most of the rain, and I think we'd be safe from any falling rock. You can see how much the wall angles out towards the water."

I looked up and saw what he meant. The cliff leaned sufficiently so that an eight-foot rain and debris shadow was created along the base of the wall.

"What about the cave?" I asked.

"It's not very deep and there's no sign of it being a burial cave. There's only some driftwood inside. If the wind picks up we could even shift the tents into the entrance and be delightfully dry."

So we set to and before long had established a good camp that was indeed dry, despite the continuing downpour. We sat in the cliff's shelter, looking out into the mist and pelting rain, and drank a late lunch of hot soup. Though the warmth was wonderful, the taste offered little to recommend it. The first of the five kayakers materialized out of the deluge and passed. Then another, and after some time, another. Then the final two. The rain intensified, the mist thickened, and they disappeared from view.

In the evening our VHF radio advised that a wet, cold front was engulfing the entire coast and that the wind was expected to rise to gale-force levels. We could well be here a day or three.

That night, tucked into my warm sleeping bag, I listened to the chorus of thousands of stones rolling in and out, directed by the infinite rhythm of the ocean swell. The backdrop of the cliff created an amplified, stereophonic sound. I drifted into the place of not quite awake, not yet asleep. Then I heard the steady pattern of a soft drumbeat: "poom-poom . . . poom-poom . . . ," all backed by the shifting roar of rubbing stones.

A spirit drummer at my door? My demand for a logical explanation dissolved the aura of magic. I unzipped the tent and looked out into the black, wet night. Heavy, swollen drops of water fell from the high cliff onto the taut skin of my kayak's cockpit cover: "poom-poom . . . poom-poom . . . " I crawled back into my bag, closed my eyes, and let the image of the spirit drummer slip back into my dreams.

The storm continued on for the next three days, and we drifted into a pattern of catnaps, reading, and eating. During one break I managed to dart out, catch a fish, and get back before the heavens reopened and dumped their next onslaught of the wet stuff. We spread our large tarp on the steep beach, the bottom edge against a long log. By the second day we'd collected enough fresh water to supply a small village!

The light show was stunning. Even at noon the dense cloud cover made it seem like nightfall; then the sun would hint at its own existence and the black sky would shift to ethereal wisps of grey and white, so brilliant it almost hurt the eyes. The mist would thin and the opposite shore would begin to materialize. Steam would rise from the wet logs, a patch of blue would appear, then the next wave of black cloud would envelope everything. It was nice to be warm and dry, sitting in the cave mouth, a bowl of hot porridge in my hands.

Later, I took my towel and soap and walked to a spot under the overhanging cliff where a natural shower had been created by the heavy rainfall. I stripped and stepped under the cold spray, washed vigorously, and climbed back into my clothing, clean and refreshed. I went to bed early and drifted off, only to be awakened by a strange "bump, bump . . . " and voices! I opened my tent door and looked out into the darkness. Two shapes staggered up the beach, dragging kayaks behind them. The boats bumped over the rocks, then were dropped. One of the shapes hauled out a large fly and the two crawled underneath. That was it. The rain increased.

～～～

We were up early next morning and decided to move on. The rain had stopped and the cloud cover appeared to be breaking up; increasing numbers of vivid blue patches appeared in the sky.

One of our neighbours crawled out from under the wet fly and dragged the smaller of the two kayaks down the rocks to the shore's edge. He leapt in and pushed off. His partner remained an inert lump under the tarp. The kayaker returned a short while later with some eight sea urchins. He'd been diving, and although in a wetsuit, appeared thoroughly chilled. The other shape moved out from under the fly. The urchins were apparently the sole item on their breakfast menu.

We were in the process of packing when one of the men shouted, "Is that you, Mike?" At 6'5" Mike is easily identifiable. He stands out in the proverbial crowd.

"Yes," he replied.

"It's me, Dan." And the two wandered over, the one still shivering from his morning swim in the chilly waters.

It turned out that Dan and his friend, Pierre, were in the process of circumnavigating Vancouver Island by kayak! They'd started out some thirty days ago from Port Hardy, had rounded Cape Scott, and were making their way down the coast. This was not a speed run, rather a trip where they were taking time to explore every nook and cranny possible. Dan was a character, exceedingly skilled but also half mad! He loved playing in "rock gardens" — those areas of wicked rock and reef where seas explode with destructive force. I measured my skill by avoiding them; Dan dove into them with a true hunger.

"We're travelling light," he said, in response to my question about their lack of a tent. "Had a bomb-proof boat built, got a fly and a wetsuit . . . basically eating what we can gather along the way. These urchins are powerful food! Eat one a day and you'll live to be eighty, with the heart of a twenty-year-old." He finished off the contents of a fourth urchin.

I was impressed with his knowledge of the west coast waters, which he'd paddled many times before. I hinted at my fears of dying off Bajo Reef or Estevan Point. "The Reef's okay," he said. "Don't believe that guidebook stuff about having to go out three or four miles to get safely around — that's true for sailboats, but not for kayaks. If you catch a high tide you'll find there's a narrow channel next to the shore that you can skim through, only inches above the rock. No problem. Now Estevan Point, that's another story. That's bad news. Boomer City is what I call it."

"Boomers" lie in lethal waters that appear safe. Underneath the surface will be a hidden rock or reef over which the majority of seas pass, giving no hint of the danger below. Now and then, however, the combination of shallow water and a larger-than-normal swell will cause the latter to suddenly steepen and crash with a "booming" destructiveness. Not a place to be at that particular moment.

Dan's words did nothing to erase my fears. Estevan sounded horrid, and his description of "cruising along just inches above rock, between reef and shore" was, I was sure, his downplayed view of a frightening rock garden. Mike and I wished them well on their circumnavigation, then finished our loading. The sun came out. A favourable weather change appeared to be happening.

We spent the best part of the morning paddling the

waters off the Nuchatlitz Islands. Although we'd not got into a big discussion about it, we were at a pivotal point. If we wanted, we could paddle inland and go down the protected side of Nootka Island, or we could head on as originally planned and go down the wild, exposed side — the side where the guidebooks warned of no landing spot for twenty-five miles, the side that also offered the chance to die off Bajo Reef.

"What do you want to do?" asked Mike.

I knocked the ball back into his court. "Don't know. What do you think?"

He countered. "Well, do you have a preference?"

And so we dallied about, making no decisions, conveying uncertainty and our underlying anxiety.

We drifted into a cove on a small island and got out. "That's a burial cave." He pointed. I looked closer and saw the small opening. Six human skulls sat on a ledge and stared back at me. It wasn't eerie. There was, though, definitely the feeling that one was in a place where one should be quiet and respectful. There was also the sense that one didn't quite know the rules. Like walking into a temple in a foreign country.

We were about to move on when we heard voices. Around the corner came the group of five we'd met on Grassy Island. They'd camped the night here and were oblivious to the fact that this was a burial island. Mike pointed it out. Suddenly the light dimmed and we looked up. To the east the sky was blue, but to the west the heavens were completely covered in the blackest of cloud. Well out to sea whitecaps danced and sheets of rain squalls could be seen. Mike and I launched and paddled fiercely for a nearby cove on Nuchatlitz Island. We landed and frantically set up our large tarp, just as the wind swept in, and the heavy rain unleashed itself with a roar.

Although only early afternoon, it was as though night had fallen. We sat and munched some cheese and crackers, then laboriously levelled two tent sites under the tarp. Then it was the eastern sky that filled with huge black clouds, as they backed up against the mountains. The rain eased, then stopped. We crawled out from under the fly, walked to a nearby bluff, and looked westward, out to the open ocean — clear, blue sky. Not a cloud!

Down came the tarp and off we went, into the choppy seas. We had yet to make a decision as to our route, so decided to paddle the three miles over to Ferrer Point on Nootka Island, "to get a sense of things." (Deep down we both knew it was "wrong" to even think of taking the inside route.) The wind came with some strength at our backs and clashed vigorously with the incoming, southerly swell. Confused seas and breaking crests resulted. Still, it was quite manageable.

As we closed in on the Point, I could feel my level of anxiety rise. We pulled alongside each other and again stared at the chart. Despite the warning in the guidebooks that there was nowhere to land over the next twenty-five miles, Mike felt there was the possibility to do so about four miles down the coast of Nootka Island. We didn't talk about what we'd do if we found it impossible to land. (This is a special technique learned in the "Ostrich School of Navigation.")

The wind eased as we rounded Ferrer Point and the sun continued to shine out of a now completely clear sky. With unspoken consensus we moved forward. The coastline was as forecast. Stark cliffs rose up, buffered by exposed rock and reef, with the occasional "boomer" thrown in, just to keep us on our toes. Suddenly the twisted remains of the Greek freighter *Treisierarcha* came into view. It had been swept onto the unforgiving shore on December 8th, 1969. Seeing the wreck made me shiver. The power that could fling such a giant of a vessel onto the rocks, and then demolish it so thoroughly, was staggering.

The wind stayed calm, but the swell was a good size and moved at a fair clip. Even if there was a potential site, I now worried the surf would be too big to allow us a chance to land. What would life be like without something to worry about?

"Well, if there's any hope, I think it'll be around that next point," shouted Mike. "Keep your fingers crossed."

We rounded the corner, snaking our way through some exposed reef. Then the cove came into view and I could have fallen to my knees in thanks. Spread out before us was the classic west coast postcard scene: a large, curved, sandy beach, complete with its own fresh-water creek, which cut deeply through the sand as it ran its course from forest to sea. Although the surf looked nasty over the main portion of the shore, the western corner was fully protected on a day such as this. I sat and watched Mike drift gently onto the sand.

What a glorious feeling to be safe and in such a paradise! The relief I felt was beyond words.

I paddled over to a large area of kelp and tried to catch a fish for dinner. It was surprisingly shallow and I kept snagging the bottom. Eventually I became frustrated and decided to pack it in. An eagle, which had been sitting high in a spruce tree, launched and drifted over me. It cried out, then returned to the same branch. In my mind I was sure it said, "Don't stop now, you fool!" I cast again, and *bam* — dinner. A large, grey rockfish gave itself up. I thanked the fish, smiled at the eagle, then turned shoreward.

The day's anxiety acted as a superb sauce for the night's dinner. I couldn't remember when cod had seemed so tender and succulent. As the sun set, we sipped some Cointreau and watched a soon-to-be-full moon rise over the forested hills, and cast its silver on the now quiet waters and soft, sandy shore.

Early in the morning near the tents we discovered two sets of very fresh wolf tracks, lending an even greater sense of magic to the place. The wind picked up, and although we were well protected in the cove, it appeared to be moving along at a good twenty-five to thirty knots out on the exposed sea. I caught a glimpse of vibrant colour through my binoculars and shouted out to Mike, "It's Dan and Pierre. They're trying to get a kite up." We sat and watched their tiny kayaks toss about in the increasing seas. Eventually they gave up on launching the kite and paddled on, unaware of our watching eyes.

It was a relaxing, hot, sun-drenched day. We explored well up the creek and also found our way into a deep burial cave. Later, we took the shower bag, which had been cooking in the day's heat, and set it up for a delightful wash. This was no primitive arrangement, rather an engineering marvel! Mike had utilized a pulley setup connected to a strategically placed pole, allowing the shower to easily be adjusted to our quite different heights.

Basking under the warm water, I contemplated what tomorrow would bring – our second encounter with potential death, Bajo Reef. The forecast was for a sunny day with gale-force winds by noon. It seemed wise to plan on a very early departure.

That night I tossed and turned for what seemed like hours, then finally slipped into a fitful sleep.

I was awakened early by Mike's voice. "It doesn't look bad out there. The forecast is for thirty-five knots later. Have a look."

I crawled out, careful not to touch the dew-soaked fly. It was cold; the sun had yet to clear the hills and touch us with its warmth. I looked out to sea. The swells were mild to moderate, with what appeared to be only a minimal wind. With some trepidation I agreed: "Yeah, looks okay."

We quickly cooked up a breakfast of hot porridge, then loaded and launched at the edge of a low tide. We angled out, intending to pass on Dan's advice of "skimming between reef and shore," and instead followed the guidebook admonition to stay "well off Bajo Reef." Before long we were several miles out to sea and the situation was decidedly unpleasant and unrewarding. Although the wind had yet to rise, the swells were now the height of medium-sized houses, and our view of the coastline was constantly obscured.

"What's that splash of white on the shore?" shouted Mike. As I rose up on the next giant swell I caught a glimpse of what he meant. "I don't know," I replied. Digging out his binoculars, he took another look from the top of the next swell. "It's a waterfall," he said. "It looks beautiful."

We sank into an incredibly deep trough. "This is crazy being this far out," said Mike. "Might as well be on a sailboat for all we're getting to see."

I hesitated a minute. Although the swells were large, there was still no sign of the forecast gale. Wouldn't we be wise to keep going and get around Bajo Reef before the wind picked up? On the other hand, the whole purpose of being in a kayak was to explore that intimate space between sea and shore. Mike was quite right; we might just as well be on a sailboat if we were going to paddle this far off the coast.

"Okay. Let's go in. We're missing the best part being way out here," I agreed.

It was a turning point in the day, and a reminder that a kayak's greatest gift is in sneaking amongst the dangerous rock and reef that keep most of humanity from exploring the wonders of this type of shoreline.

Soon we were in beds of kelp so thick that the paddle would hardly penetrate. Using the blade as a blunt-ended pole, I pushed my craft across what seemed to be an endless field of kelp, so dense I wondered if I might have even tried walking on it! Needless to say, the effect of shallower waters and such a forest of growth reduced the house-sized swells to a flat millpond.

What a beach! A long, sandy shore, with a brilliant, large waterfall cascading into the deepest part of the cove. And more fresh wolf tracks. We sat and quietly savoured lunch in this primordial paradise.

"You know, it's the Labour Day long weekend," I said. "This is the Monday when the millions return home, bumper to bumper."

Mike smiled. We basked in our good fortune. "I'm glad you saw that flash of white," I said. "It was the right thing to come in."

We refilled our water bags under the splendid falls, then eyed wicked Bajo Reef. The monster swells exploded violently on the barely hidden shoals, which extended three miles out to sea.

"Well, we'll see if Dan's advice about skimming along

betwixt reef and shore is valid," said Mike. "If he's right, our timing is impeccable. It's almost high tide."

We launched, this time paddling practically on top of the shoreline, and picked our way delicately amongst the rocks. Dan was right. And luck was with us. We literally floated over boulders, which in some places lay only inches below the surface. The swell was virtually eliminated by the vastness of Bajo Reef and we paddled in waters upon which not a ripple stirred.

As we reached the far side of the reef, and once again found ourselves in open waters, we began to feel the effect of the increasing afternoon winds.

"It's probably about twenty-five knots," said Mike. "Want to try the kite?" I nodded.

We rafted up and dug out one of our parafoil kites. It was a pain to launch, but once up, what a thrill! Wind and swell were both with us. White foam spewed from our bows as we raced down the front of the large seas. Soon, however, the waves increased dramatically and began breaking.

"Time to pull the kite in or we're going to find ourselves playing submarine," I shouted.

"Yeah, it is getting a little dicey alright," replied Mike. And so we reeled in.

We paddled on at a good clip, admiring the large number of sea caves that had appeared along the shore once past Bajo Reef. Sea otters were also in abundance, lying on their backs, adjacent to the many beds of kelp along the way. There seemed a law that stated: "Once Michael has gone to all the trouble of removing his spray skirt, pulling his good camera out of the waterproof box, and adjusting the telescopic lens, whatever creature he wishes to photograph shall dive under the ocean's surface." I was sure I already had a good dozen pictures of rippled water and invisible otters to my credit.

"There it is." Mike pointed to the distant village at Friendly Cove, which marked the bottom of Nootka Island. We paddled on and soon passed the village and the lighthouse, and made our way into the Provincial Recreation

Area at Santa Gertrudis Cove. The sailing guides had indicated it was a "beautiful cove," but it soon became obvious that it all depended upon one's point of view. Perhaps, after sailing in house-sized swells all day, the protected waters of this cove would seem a delight. Compared to the beaches we'd camped on, however, it seemed a most depressing place with virtually nowhere to site a tent. It had been a challenging and grand day, and this was not the place to end it.

"Got enough energy to cross over Nootka Sound?" asked Mike.

I looked at the chart and did a quick calculation. "If we can get into one of those coves below Burdwood Point, we'll have paddled over thirty miles today. Of course I've got the energy! Besides, it's so idyllic out here, with all the pink whales cavorting about, and I particularly like the pulsating purple auras around the eagles. Naw, I'm not tired." Mike laughed and we pushed on, across the Sound, to the far shore.

The extra paddle was well worth it, for we managed to sneak into a perfect little cove complete with shell beach, creek, and access to both morning and evening sun.

I crawled out of my kayak and only then did it hit me what a long day we'd put in, and how exhausted I was. By the time we'd set up camp and eaten, my eyes would hardly stay open. The red sun sank into the ocean and the moon rose up behind our tents. I could stay awake no longer.

~~~~~

Despite my fatigue, or perhaps because of it, I could not settle into a deep sleep. I tossed and turned. Suddenly I was awakened by a roaring giant that rammed my tent, then tried to pick it up and fling it down the beach. Only the weight of my personal gear and my own body kept things on the ground. My mind cleared and I soon realized that there was a steady stream of powerful wind gusts slamming our cove. It was a strange feeling to be lying in the little shelter, to hear the approaching roar of a gust, then to feel the tent, frame and all, dance about in an effort to get up and run away. As each gust approached I could feel my whole body tense in an effort to hold the tent in place. Eventually, during a lull, I crawled out and dragged two heavy logs along either side of my little abode and fastened things more securely.

At dawn, Mike announced that, what with yesterday's paddle and the night's wrestle with the wind, he had no intention of doing anything other than resting today. I breathed a sigh of relief! "Well, if you feel you need it," I replied.

There was no answer.

And so it was a day of rest, eating, bathing, and napping. The high pressure system held. The sun shone down, the wind fell to a refreshing breeze.

A few days later found us camped only about five miles away on tiny Escalante Island. We'd started out for Estevan Point. Dan's warning that the area was "boomer city and lethal" proved to be entirely correct. It was an area that demanded caution and a good deal of concentration. At one point we'd taken our attention off the horizon and turned to watch several grey whales feeding in nearby shallow waters. "Oh-oh. I don't like the look of that at all," said Mike. I looked up. Over the mountains and hills, and closing in from the ocean, was the densest of flowing white fog. One of my ultimate nightmares would be to get caught in this blender of rock, reef, and breaking seas with *no visibility*. The magic of whales feeding so close by quickly vanished, and we cast our eyes about for a possible landing spot.

"What about the little island we passed back there?" I said. "It looked like it had a small shell beach."

"It seems the best bet," Mike agreed. "Let's have a look."

The menacing fog slipped down the hills and out over the water. The whales dissolved. We turned and paddled with a fervour. And thus our arrival on Escalante Island.

The little white beach was a tiny gem bordered by turquoise waters. We calculated the possible high tide line and found we had a glorious couple of feet to spare. There was no room for error, or high winds. The fog wrapped us in its shadowy vapours, creating a magical world of shifting forms. Nearby we heard the blowing of invisible whales.

During the superb evening meal of "Sheehan Chili" (a 9+ on the "Escalante Dining Out Scale"), the fog suddenly melted and the hills and mountains rose up. The ocean was flat. We raised our glasses, and with the last of the wine, asked for a favourable passage around Estevan Point. That night, at about 1:00 AM, the high tide came to within a foot of my tent door, then gracefully retreated.

<hr />

We awoke early, our anxiety high. Today was the last of the lethal "this is where I might die" obstacles. The sky was completely overcast with low, thick cloud, adding a menacing tone to the air. The wind was mild. The radio reported winds of only six to ten knots at Estevan. We launched into "boomer city." Again a feeding grey whale passed by, this time so close that I had an anxious moment and prayed that all its navigational senses were in good order.

Despite the calm winds, the area was exceedingly dangerous. Huge, fast-moving swells roared in, exploding left and right on hidden rock and reef. Mike was superb at avoiding not only the obvious dangers, but also in noting the subtle indicators . . . a swell that rose a little higher than others, sudden swirling and frothing . . . all telling of nasty stuff below!

I sat about twenty yards behind Mike, playing my own learning game, picking out hypothetical routes and seeing if they coincided with the course we took. If not, I still followed, but kept my eye on the route I might have gone if alone. It was a nerve-racking, but wonderful learning experience.

We passed Split Cape and came upon an immense rock garden that carried well out to sea. We tried an inside run, dangerously close to shore. There was no way through and we had to retreat, then head out around the notorious Perez Rocks. The dense beds of kelp prevented the seas from breaking; nonetheless, they were astoundingly steep. At times I felt my bow was pointed for a launch into the heavens. I paddled arduously through the thick kelp . . . up, up . . . then the swell would pass under me at a frightening speed and a million coils of kelp would appear in the shallow waters of the trough below.

The gods obviously felt we didn't need any more of a challenge and so they held off on increasing the wind or allowing the offshore fog to roll in. We wound our way through even more rock, then drifted into the calm and protected waters of Homias Cove, the site of a now abandoned Native village. The cloud cover started to break and the light became particularly soft and gentle. I took a most-needed pee, and drank copious quantities of water. We sat and enjoyed a well-earned lunch.

Back into the sea we spied the flickering light of Estevan Point, emanating from what is the tallest lighthouse on the coast. A Coastguard helicopter approached from behind and flew low over us, settling in at the keeper's house. Lunchtime?

Conditions could not have been more ideal. There was still little wind and the current was slack. Still, the rock and shoal extended well out to sea, and the height of the incoming swells easily erased my view of the 125-foot-high lighthouse.

At one point we stopped and pondered the course ahead. Even Mike felt we'd be wise to avoid the minefield before us. "We're probably better off going out a bit further than trying to find a way through that stuff," he said. I couldn't have agreed more. Mike undid his spray skirt, pulled out his good camera from the waterproof case, and took some shots of the lighthouse. We paddled on. A deafening, crashing roar came from behind us. We whirled around. Less than thirty yards to the rear, where we'd paused, contemplated, and taken photos, I saw the remnants of a huge exploding swell. My God! Directly where we'd sat! Thank you, my lucky eagle feather . . . thank you, thank you!

Our different natures immediately came to the fore. Mike began calculating how shallow the water must have been to create a breaking sea that high. I, on the other hand, simply kept muttering, "I guess it wasn't time for us to die yet."

The kelp was now thicker than I'd ever seen. So thick I

wanted to get out and drag my kayak over it. The clouds broke, then vanished, and a hot sun beat down. Eventually we reached Matlahaw Point and paused to watch some humungous explosions of swell on the reef. And this on a good day! We gave it a wide birth.

The wind suddenly strengthened at our backs, and soon was blowing a good twenty-five knots, yet the seas stayed small. Ideal conditions, in my mind. We literally screamed across the surface, barely dipping our paddles in the water. I could do this all day! We shot by the channel marker, as it rocked in the swell, making its loud, moaning sound. It was covered with sea birds, and a huge sea lion lay fast asleep on its steel surface, unaware of our presence only a few feet away.

In less than an hour we reached Hesquiat Point and began searching for a landing spot. The dumping surf was powerful stuff — "obliteration" was written all over its surface.

We paddled into the deeper recesses of the harbour and checked out possible spots for the night. It didn't feel like an uplifting place. The mountains were scarred from intense logging; there was no sense of open ocean swell, and a shallow shoreline would make for a long carry on the morning's low tide. We turned and headed back out to the exposed coast, past the seas crashing on the rock beaches. The chart we had was of a poor scale, but Mike's articulate eyes noted a couple of possible options a few miles further on. Soon we passed steep cliffs and some magnificent sea caves. It was tempting to contemplate landing. The ever-present image of my kayak as an overripe watermelon dropping on the rocks quickly clarified the outcome of any attempt we might make. Still, it was breathtakingly beautiful, and most enticing.

We paddled a narrow corridor between two large seastacks and startled a sea lion we'd not seen. It flung itself off the dry ledge into the water some ten feet below. Out of nowhere a lone eagle approached, drifted above us, then turned sharply and disappeared behind the next rocky outcropping.

"That'll be it!" I shouted.

"That's what I hope," Mike answered.

It was! The tide was perfect. Higher, and the surf would have been dumping on the steep beach; lower, and we'd be in the land of large boulders. As it was, all that was required was a cautious one-at-a-time approach onto a tiny patch of sand. The cove was beautifully protected and surrounded by an abundance of sea caves. A fresh creek, from Kanim Lake, emptied into the ocean. We found cougar tracks and scat along the high tide line. On the more benign side, Mike lifted a piece of wood to find mamma field mouse and her babies all tucked into a soft, moss nest. He gently lowered the wood and spent the rest of our days here keeping them amply supplied with fresh cheese and peanut butter. The cheese won out, hands down.

<center>~~~~~</center>

That night we sat sipping Cointreau, watching the sun sink into a massive offshore fog bank, and contemplated the fact that the journey was almost done. We'd survived the three lethal "this is where I will die" encounters, and once again I'd been shown how pathetically unproductive worrying can be.

Travelling the full distance had been a challenge well worth taking, but it had become abundantly clear that this was not the style of trip I enjoyed most. It became too goal-oriented, with constant pressure to push on while the going was good. It was more important for me to learn the wisdom of "rushing slowly." With the journey's end now in sight, we paused, and shifted into a lower gear that was quite delightful.

Eventually the last night arrived. It was tinged with a sense of sadness. The time and distance had gone so quickly; in a few days I'd be back at work, and these past weeks would be but nourishing memories.

CATCHES-FEATHER

CATCHES-FEATHER

IN THE MID-SEVENTIES I moved to a little shack by
the water's edge on a two-hundred-acre farm in the Gulf
Islands. I had no electricity, plumbing, phone, or water. It
was *very* basic. It was also one of the most beautiful places
I've ever lived. I was there for seven years, and for a portion of that time I acted as caretaker for the family who
owned the chickens, the sheep, the property. Over the
years that have followed we have remained good friends,
and they have very kindly allowed me to continue to make
use of the shack.

On this particular occasion my wife was at work for a
three-day stretch. My five-year-old daughter and I decided
to pack food, sleeping bags and kayak, and head over to
the cabin on Saltspring Island. I tore home after work,
loaded the gear into my ten-year-old station wagon, and off

we went, catching the last ferry from Swartz Bay to Fulford Harbour. By the time we arrived at the shack, darkness had settled in. I turned off the car motor.

"It's so quiet," whispered a tired Camila.

"Let's go and see if the beach is still here," I said.

It was a clear night, with a sharply defined crescent moon artfully hung in the sky; tall cedars and fir framed it on either side. The shack, a board and batten structure built of rough-sawn timber, sat directly on the edge of a small white shell beach. The front portion of the cabin rested on sturdy pilings. Once, on a high, high tide, coupled with strong winds, the ocean had deftly removed these supports! Fortunately, the shack had only listed, instead of collapsing, and I'd been able to make the necessary repairs.

A narrow path led down the side, and we followed it to the protected little beach. Not a breath of wind this evening.

"I wonder if the water still sparkles," said Camila, remembering another visit when the ocean had been thick with glowing bio-luminescence. She grabbed a large rock and threw it into the water . . . then another and another . . . then handfuls of pebbles and sand. The water glittered and flashed with a greenish-white florescence. She laughed, grabbed a big stick, and began stirring it back and forth, creating a brilliant, glowing swirl. Chuckling, and lost in her enjoyment, she stepped in further, to the point where water slipped in over the top of her boots.

"Oh-oh, I think I went too deep, Dad! But it's okay. Don't worry."

I laughed. "Come on, we've got to get our stuff inside." She turned and we walked back up the trail to the car and began unloading our gear. I unlocked the shack door. It was damp and cool inside.

"I'll help get a fire going, Dad."

"Good, it'll be nice to get the place warmed up. Let me put some lights on first."

I'd wired the shack with a couple of plug-ins and light sockets for a twelve-volt system and had run the wiring out to where the cars normally parked. It was a simple matter each visit to connect the wire to the car battery and *presto*, instant light. Once back in the shack, I also lit a coal-oil lamp, then turned my attention to firing up the wood stove.

Camila was a great help, scrunching up newspaper and placing small pieces of cedar on top. Soon the fire was crackling away. We stepped back and looked up through the large skylights and saw the smoke pour out of the chimney and across the face of the moon.

"Okay. You figure out where you want your bed and let's get the sleeping bags undone. It's late," I said.

Camila climbed up five steps to a roomy loft, surrounded on three sides by large windows.

"I'm sleeping here." She pointed to the window. "And I want to make a tent over me, please."

So we quickly got to it . . . put a foam on the floor and made a tent out of blankets. Before long she was curled up in her down bag and fast asleep.

I set up my own sleeping quarters in the far corner, turned the twelve-volt light off, and sat by the crackling fire, sipping a glass of wine. The quiet was broken only by the peaceful sound of waves gently lapping on the shore. The glow from the coal-oil lamp was soothing, as was the wine. Later I filled the firebox, damped the stove down, and crawled into my sleeping bag. I could hear the occasional sound of seals and otters on the water. Then I, too, drifted off.

~~~~~

Camila woke at first light.

"It's morning, Dad."

"It's still early," I muttered.

"I need to go to the bathroom."

"Well, go," I said. "You know where the outhouse is."

"You come with me. It's scary. The hole's too deep."

With great reluctance I dragged myself out of bed and escorted her up the little white-shell path to the post and beam outhouse, complete with large window.

"Don't go away," she said firmly.

It was a beautiful morning. The sun was only just coming up over distant Galiano Island. There was no wind.

I'd installed a three-burner propane stove in the shack that had originally inhabited an old van of mine. I turned it on, and Camila and I soon had the hotcakes cooking. We stacked them up, buttered them, then drenched them with maple syrup. I put everything on a tray, including a hot cafe au lait, and we traipsed through the grass and into the forest, following a winding path that took us to a tiny cove we affectionately called the "little bay." As corny as it sounds, it can only be described as "a place of good feeling."

We each found a comfortable rock, with good back support, and settled in. The early morning sun shone directly on us. The pancakes were wonderful, the coffee perfect. The calmness was all-pervasive.

"Are we going to have fish or crab for dinner?" asked Camila.

"Well, I think we should try to catch some fish, have them for dinner, and put the heads in the crab trap to catch tomorrow night's dinner. What do you think?"

"Good idea," she replied. "Let's make a picnic lunch and go over there and see if we can catch some fish and maybe see some seals." She pointed towards Wallace Island.

We cleaned up, made lunch, and then unloaded my single kayak from the roof of the car. Camila was still *just* small enough to squeeze in the cockpit with me. She sat on a special piece of foam, and I'd made a two-holed spray skirt that we used in the event of choppy or rough waters. She'd reached the age where she loved to hold her hands on the paddle, then try to make us go as fast as possible. She dearly wanted to do it herself, but she lacked the strength. She was stubborn, though, and constantly insisted on trying. The weight of the paddle was such that the moment she dropped the blade into the water she was almost pulled overboard. I had to be careful that she didn't inadvertently cause a capsize.

We loaded up and made ourselves comfortable, looking like two stuffed dolls with our lifejackets on. I pushed off and we slid into the clear, calm waters. It was warm. A little sunscreen was in order, as were the sunglasses. We paddled towards a reef about a mile and a half away, across Trincomali Channel. Over the years I'd had good luck catching fish there.

"I think a lingcod would be good, Dad, then we don't have to worry about those sharp spikes like the other ones have." She referred to the spines on the rockfish we often caught. "But you gotta bonk it good, Dad, 'cause I don't want those sharp teeth in the kayak with us." She was right. The ling had no spikes to worry about, but their teeth were indeed another matter.

We paddled the distance with ease, then got out the collapsible rod and set things up, using a yellow-green version of a lure known as a "buzz-bomb."

"Let me do it, Dad."

"Well, just a sec. Let me cast and see how deep it is."

I flicked my wrist and the lure flew out and pierced the water adjacent to a kelp bed that ran alongside the reef. I let the line slide out until it suddenly stopped, indicating the lure had hit bottom. I snapped the bale shut and wound the line in, to a point where I guessed the "bomb" to be a foot or so above the bottom. I gently lifted the tip of the rod about two to three feet, then lowered it quickly. In my mind's eye I could see the buzz-bomb fluttering downward.

Bam! Something hit it. I snapped the rod upwards. Yes, there was something big on it.

"Would you hold on to this?" I said, handing the rod to Camila. "I need to fix something."

She let go of the paddle she'd been diligently caretaking and started to lift the tip of the rod in imitation of what I'd done. It immediately began a jerking motion and was pulled down in dramatic fashion. The line screamed out, then stopped.

"I've got something, I've got something!" she shouted.

She was so excited. Her little jaw was set. She tried to wind the reel. It wouldn't move.

"It must be stuck on the bottom," she whispered.

Whizzzzzzz! The line suddenly sang out again, then stopped.

"I bet it's a big ling," I said.

"Help me wind it," she asked.

So we started. Lift the rod up, then wind it in slowly as we lower . . . make sure we don't drift into the kelp . . . stay away from the submerged rock . . .

Eventually, after several more downward runs we pulled the fish alongside. It *was* a big ling.

"Don't forget, Dad. I want it really, really bonked before we put it in the kayak." This was said *most* firmly.

I could see the hook was well set and there was no risk of losing the fish. I pulled out my long fillet knife, encased in a reinforced sheath, homemade exactly for "bonking" purposes.

"Hold the rod," I said to Camila. I held the line taut and struck the fish twice, then a third time. It quivered, then was still. I removed the hook and placed the ling in a bag in the cockpit.

"Is it dead?" asked Camila. I nodded. "Does everything really have its time to die, Dad?"

"Yes. . . . "

The moment of life and death issues passed as the wise little voice said, "Is it lunchtime yet?"

We paddled over to a series of rocky outcroppings by the Secretary Islands, where Camila had previously pointed out a number of bleached logs.

"Are those really logs?" I asked.

"Sure."

"Well, let's just stop and take a closer look," I said.

She stared. And then in a voice filled with curiosity stated, "I think one moved!" We drifted closer. One of the logs lifted its head.

"Dad, they're seals, not logs!"

And she was right. About twenty to twenty-five seals slid off the rocks, then assembled in assorted groups behind and alongside us. One rose up not a foot from our bow, looking the other way. It suddenly turned, and with a startled slap on the surface, dove quickly into the depths and away. We drifted for fifteen minutes watching the seals. Some of the younger ones swam directly under us, their light-coloured bellies visible in the clear, calm waters. High in the sky, over the island, four eagles soared in an upward spiral with nary a flap of wing.

"Still hungry?" I asked.

"Yes. And I need to pee, too."

We landed on the shore. Camila wandered off to pee while I set to filleting the ling. Halfway through the task, I sensed a little presence beside me. I looked up. Camila stood stark-naked at my elbow.

"What are you doing?" I asked.

"Well, I didn't want to get any pee on my clothes so I took my boots and socks off, and then my pants, too. Then I thought I might want to swim so I took off my shirt."

It all made sense; still, it was the fall . . . on the other hand, it was an awfully warm day.

"Can I touch the fish?" asked Camila. She leaned over and rested her finger on the cheek, the eye, and the skin. "What's that?" she asked, pointing at the belly.

"It's the stomach. Let's see what it ate for breakfast," I said. I cut the sac open and out came several tiny critters.

"They're dead little crabs!" she exclaimed. "What a yucky breakfast!"

I sat on a warm rock and ate my picnic lunch. Camila wandered about, munching her favourite sandwich of peanut butter and jam.

"I think this is a really special place," she said. "It's got the neatest beach glass. I'm going to take some back for Mom, too."

For the next few hours she crouched, moving slowly about, finding pieces of well-worn translucent glass, shells, and *special* rocks. Her hunt covered an area of less than four yards square. After awhile she piled some of her collection on the towel next to me, then walked over to the water's edge and slid down a smooth wet rock into the chilly ocean. She played and splashed until I could see her whole body was shivering, and I had to tell her to get out.

"But I'm having fun," she replied.

"I just want you to stay out awhile to warm up."

"But I'm not cold."

"Look at you! You're shivering."

"Well maybe I am, but I'm not cold."

"Out!" I demanded.

Then she was back to scrounging on the beach, totally absorbed. I thought of a line spoken by Colonel Potter on the television series "M*A*S*H": "If you're not where you are, then you're nowhere."

Eventually the time came to leave. We packed her special goodies, she dressed, and we put on our life jackets. We squeezed into the cockpit, pushed off, and paddled very slowly amongst the rocks, eyeing the basking seals. Camila pointed her tiny finger at two eagles perched high in a tree.

"One's a grownup — the one with the white head. The one that's all brown is still a kid."

"SQUAWK! SQUAWK!"

We both nearly fell overboard. A large heron spread its wings, crying out as it launched from a nearby tree into the air. It angled upward, then, unexpectedly, it brushed against one of the highest branches.

"Look!" whispered Camila.

A lone feather had been dislodged. It didn't drop. Instead it floated, ever so slowly, and twisted like a propeller on a child's beanie. It began to drift out over the water. We started to paddle to where we thought it might land. Then, it seemed to hesitate and actually catch a gentle updraft, all the while, turning, turning. . . .

"It's going into the forest," gasped Camila, despair in her voice.

Then it moved again, back out over the water. We did our own little dance underneath . . . paddle to the right, then back a bit, now to the left. So, so slowly, the feather turned, then gracefully made its way downward, the sun glancing off its beautiful blue-grey colour. It hovered, moved closer and closer . . . then gently settled into Camila's outstretched hand.

That night Camila lay close to sleep, snuggled up in her warm bed. She held the feather beside her.

"Tell the end of the story again," she asked, "about our adventure today."

"Well," I said, "after the little girl caught the heron feather, her father told her that from now on she had a most special name . . . it was Catches-Feather."

Camila looked up. "I like that, Daddy, only you missed the best part."

"I did?"

"Yes . . . when the feather floated down it made the shape of a 'C' in the sky." She drew a big "C" in the air with her tiny finger. "You know what I mean — a 'C' for Camila."

She smiled and closed her eyes.

A SINKING FEELING

A *SINKING* FEELING

~~~

THE WIND HOWLED and the seas reared and hurled themselves onto the rugged coast. For the fourth straight day we concluded it would be suicidal to even contemplate launching our kayaks from the protection of our idyllic cove. Two weeks ago we'd set out from Klaskino Inlet. We'd leisurely explored both the East Creek and Klaskino River estuaries, then made our way out and along the northern side of the Brooks Peninsula. On the tenth day we'd pulled into a tiny beach only a short distance from Cape Cook. Then the wind had increased to gale- and storm-force levels, and we'd wisely chosen to stay shore-bound. Today we would try hiking to the Cape, with the hope of calmer winds tomorrow.

~~~

Next morning dawned bright and clear. The clouds that had unleashed overnight showers were nowhere to be seen.

I heard the 5:45 AM weather report coming from Mike's tent. It indicated reasonable winds along the west coast, with the critical exception of the Brooks: "Solander Island, twenty-five-knot winds from the northwest, gusting to thirty-five."

"Take a look," said Mike. "It doesn't seem very windy out there at all."

"Oh yeah, and I suppose the guy on the radio is just trying to trick us," I mumbled to myself.

I crawled out of the tent and surveyed the scene before me. As always, the waters of the little cove were relatively calm; beyond, the swells seemed large, but there was only a mild wind and no sign of whitecaps. Still, I was very nervous. Thirty-five-knot winds anywhere was frightening, and I questioned the sanity of venturing onto the water.

"You really think it's wise to head out?" I asked.

"I think we'd be smart to skip breakfast and go for it before another system moves in and we end up spending the rest of our lives here," replied Mike. "It certainly doesn't look like it's blowing more than ten knots out there right now, and we're only a mile or so from the Cape."

"Going for it" referred to getting out and around Cape Cook, past Solander Island, and down the other side of the Brooks to the next feasible landing spot.

Although we'd paddled around the Cape before, we'd always been blessed with exceptionally good conditions. Both of us were all too aware of its nasty reputation for fierce weather — calling it the "Cape of Storms" was not a misnomer. It was thus with a high degree of anxiety that we broke camp and hauled our gear and craft down to the water's edge. We packed quickly, both lost in our separate thoughts.

I steadied Mike's kayak while he climbed in, then gave it a good shove. I waited, detected a lull in the small surf, and eased my heavily laden craft into the shallows. I launched and quickly paddled for the magical area beyond possible breaking seas. Alas, the last swell I needed to pass rolled smoothly across my deck, then gently poured into my lap, cold and wet. I reached down, grabbed the sponge, and soaked up the few cups of water sloshing about.

After putting on my spray skirt, I followed Mike through the cove's narrow and dangerous exit, my adrenaline pumping as I carefully eyed the rocks on left and right. The seas were confused and large; I had not the slightest desire to get flipped over or drawn into one of the cavernous holes created by the powerful surge. Once through, however, the swells proved to be regular and nicely spaced. We paddled out of the shade into the warmth of the sun, and set course for the Cape.

"You got the brush?" asked Mike.

"Brush? What are you talking about?"

"You know, the little wooden brush for cleaning the dishes."

"No, I don't have it. Why would I?"

"I left it for you to wash your cup," he said.

"I didn't use my cup," I replied.

Mike stopped. This little brush had been with him a long, long time. Still, there comes a point where things have to be put into a larger perspective.

"It's a most sacred place to have left it," I offered. "I would suggest we not risk damaging ourselves, our craft, or losing this wonderful window of good weather by even hesitating to contemplate a return."

"I haven't seen another like it," he replied.

I pretended not to hear and pushed on. A few strokes later I cast a quick glance over my shoulder and with a great sense of relief saw he was following. Thank God he'd decided it was okay to abandon the brush!

We snugged in closer to the shore to avoid some boomers and were able to confirm that on our arduous hike of the previous day, we had indeed stood on the actual Cape!

"That's it!" I shouted. "That's where we were."

The swells were big, with only a few whitecaps in evidence.

"Considering the winds of the last few days, I can't believe our good fortune," said Mike.

I nodded in agreement. We paused, took some photos, then turned towards Solander Island, a mile distant. To my surprise, Mike stayed well behind, as he'd done ever since leaving the cove. This was unlike our normal routine, which would usually see him pulling well ahead, then pausing until I'd caught up. Ah well, it was a change, and although I found it a bit nerve-racking, it was a good challenge to be the one picking the way.

Solander was as pristine as I remembered. Sea birds rested on the steep cliffs and the roar of Stellar sea lions could be heard from the far side. The wind increased and I became anxious to move on. I paused and waited for Mike.

"Want to go around the outside of the island?" he shouted.

"What?" I exclaimed. "Are you nuts? The wind's picking up, the seas are getting rougher, and the gods are wondering why we're dallying around out here. Tell you what, I'll compromise. Let's paddle out around the end and see what it's like on the other side."

And so we turned from our course and headed in the direction of Japan. As we rounded the far tip of Solander, the seas became larger and came at us from every direction. Now the mammoth sea lions were visible, roaring and posturing from their perch on the jagged rocks.

"I think we'd be wise to contemplate turning around and moving on!" I shouted. Mike vanished in a gigantic trough, then he appeared, the front third of his boat completely out of the water. A swell suddenly broke next to me and the white foam smothered my kayak. For a moment I must have seemed a bizarre apparition . . . a half-man rising out of the water, paddle in hand, and no visible means of flotation. I marvelled at how seaworthy my craft was; I'd hardly needed to brace despite the power of the breaking wave. Again I saw Mike's bow rise out of another hollow in which he'd been almost engulfed. "Strange how differently our kayak's ride," I thought. I turned to matters at hand and shouted again, "Time to move on?" Mike grinned and nodded in agreement.

We returned to the lush, protected side of Solander, where the waters were less confused. We paused and took time to drift, basking in the island's untamed beauty. A couple of tufted puffins drifted into a landing. A wave suddenly broke across my stern, startling me. I looked northwards and saw that the ocean's surface was now almost completely covered in whitecaps.

We took more photos, then turned and headed towards the next possible landing spot some four to five miles away. Again I seemed to easily pull away from Mike. The wind and breaking seas were at my back and I moved quickly along, my eyes sharply peeled for hidden rock that I knew lay between us and a safe arrival.

What a day! Surely things would have seemed little changed three or four hundred years ago at this very spot. Wild seas, rugged shoreline, and not a hint of human presence. Fortunately, the weather had not yet crossed the line into real danger. Still, it was enough to heighten all my senses. I felt finely tuned, everything well honed. The sun bounced off the pure white of the breaking seas. It was exhilarating.

I turned to look for Mike. I couldn't see him! How stupid of me, paddling along in my own daydreams and looking only ahead. Had he capsized? My eyes swept the whitecapped ocean. Nothing!

Ah! There he was! Just his head, now the bow of his kayak. What was taking so long?

Normally, Mike and I got along exceedingly well. The number of serious arguments we'd had over the many years of paddling could be counted on one hand with lots of fingers left over. I was thus surprised to find myself getting angrier and angrier inside. "What's with this guy! Why, oh why, is he dawdling? It's absolute foolishness. Here we've got the perfect opportunity for getting around the Cape and now he's choosing to contemplate his navel as the winds get stronger and the seas rougher and rougher." Part of me recognized that my anger was actually a reflection of my own increasing fear and anxiety. This awareness, however, did nothing to put me at ease.

I paused, drank some water, and munched on a granola bar. Mike approached, but ever so slowly. Eventually he pulled alongside, looking tired and worried.

"I don't know what's wrong," he shouted. "I can't keep up to you. It feels like I'm sinking."

My head whirled around and I stared at his kayak. A swell passed underneath and his bow rose well into the air. The back half of his kayak disappeared completely under water. "My God, you are!" I replied.

"Maybe I just put too much weight in the stern?" Mike offered, knowing this was not the case.

Water was obviously making its way into the rear compartment. Thankfully, the bulkhead behind his seat was holding. It would be almost certain disaster if the cockpit filled as well. Then the craft would slowly sink while shifting to a vertical position. Only the bow would stay above water, making it virtually impossible to reenter, especially with conditions as rough as this. "Cleopatra's needle" was the term that aptly described this potential nightmare.

I paddled alongside, my eyes seeking an obvious crack or hole. Nothing was visible. The coastline was littered with ugly rocks and reef. The thought of attempting an emergency landing was out of the question.

"You got enough energy to keep paddling?" I asked. A stupid question! It must have been exhausting to have paddled this heavy, totally unbalanced barge all day; fear, necessity — call it what you will — obviously provided enough fuel to continue on. Thank God Mike was such a powerful paddler. A weaker individual would have been in a real quandary.

Mike dug in and urged the half-sunken vessel along. I racked my brain for possible rescue measures in the event that his craft continued to sink. We both had paddle floats and inflatable "sea-seats." The latter were inner-tube-like items that folded into a compact pouch on the back of our life jackets. If all else failed, maybe we could somehow or other inflate and lash these things under or alongside his stern. Even if we could, would he be able to make any progress with that much drag? I doubted it. I thought of lashing my bow to his stern and creating a mammoth double kayak with a kink in the middle.

I kept tucked alongside as Mike paddled the rough waters with amazing energy.

"It looks like the rear hold has absorbed all the water it can," I said. "You don't seem to be sinking any deeper." I stared intently at his waterline.

"Look out!" Mike shouted. "A rock!" I'd been so preoccupied with eyeballing his sinking kayak that I'd paid no attention to the course ahead. Directly in front of me lay a partially submerged rock. Arrgh! The last thing we needed now was for me to get pummelled to pieces. I quickly shifted course. A glance at the shoreline showed we were making good progress, due mainly to the strong winds and following seas.

Ahead lay the dangerous waters off Banks Reef.

"This is where that solo canoeist got demolished," I offered.

"A most uplifting thought," replied Mike. I caught a glimpse of a smile on his face. He knew he was winning the battle. We paused.

"Tired?" I asked.

"Exhausted," he replied.

Ahead two seastacks rose up out of the rough seas. Atop one sat a lone eagle. My lucky omen! It lifted off the craggy peak and flew between the pillars, then turned shoreward over the rock-laced entrance, towards our intended landing spot. "That's the course!" I shouted. And so we followed.

Fifteen minutes later we sat outside the mild surf. Then Mike moved his waterlogged craft forward, through the white foam, and ground to a halt on the sandy shore. He dragged himself out of the cockpit and walked to the bow. Grabbing the toggle, he tried to pull the kayak further up the beach; not so much as one inch could he budge the weighted beast. As the swell receded, we saw water gush from a four-inch slit in the keel.

I landed, and we began the arduous task of unloading Mike's rear hold. Everything was soaked. Salt water had found its way into all his waterproof bags and boxes. Even double-bagged food was wet. We spread everything out on the beach, under the blazing sun, including the dried blue-berries and beans, now somewhat soggy. Our fortune was in abundance. That afternoon proved to be the hottest of the trip. All of Mike's gear dried, including the VHF radio, which had become *damp* despite being carried in the extra expensive "drybox."

Later, after regaining some of our dissipated energy, we examined Mike's overturned kayak in detail. It appeared the culprit was a small, sharp-edged pebble we found embedded in the hull. We surmised that upon landing on the north side of the Brooks, in our little cove adjacent to the Cape, this tiny stone had pierced Mike's well-worn keel. A nudge up the beach by the surf, with the weight of the fully laden craft on this sharp point, caused a neat surgical incision about four inches long. After our launch this morning, water must have poured in, then slowly continued to accumulate as it penetrated various "dry" bags and boxes.

By early evening we'd repaired the gash with magical duct tape and an epoxy-styled caulking. The food dried and the amount we had to abandon was minuscule. As dusk settled over us, we poured a couple of tall glasses of cool white wine, and sat watching the powerful swells roar by our protected cove.

"I don't believe it," said Mike, standing up and pointing seaward. "What an end to the day!"

My eyes followed the direction of his hand. An almost-full moon hung in the August sky, and below, moving gracefully through the rough waters towards Solander Island, were four killer whales. We raised our glasses in silent appreciation to the unseen spirits.

"Ah, but it is good to be alive," said Mike.

DAY OF TWO SUNSETS

DAY OF TWO SUNSETS

~~~◦~~~

THE MORNING SUN rose from behind the distant peaks and struck our dew-soaked tents about 7:00 AM. The tide was exceedingly low and the beach had been swept clean by the night's high waters. I ambled down to a spot where the sand was hard and flat, though still in the shade; it was always a joy to walk on ground devoid of any human print. Out by a nearby reef, hordes of gulls went berserk over a ball of feed that swirled in the water below.

I started my morning ritual of tai chi, a routine I'd begun some twenty years ago. I found it a wonderful way to slowly stretch and begin the day. As my old Chinese teacher had said, way back in the beginning: "Michael, you always go fast in your life, like hummingbird. That okay if you calm inside and breathe deep. If you fast inside and no breathe deep, then inside and outside go all over the place.

You remember: Inside calm, deep breathe, then okay you be like hummingbird outside." Partway through the 108 movements, the rising sun washed over me.

While doing the sequence of motions my mind always tended to drift to a variety of concerns and plans; on a journey like this I often worried about the "what ifs" that lay ahead. Tai chi, on the other hand, provided a tool for being in the "now," by gently drawing my mind back to the movements and breathing . . . a meditation in motion. As a way of tricking myself into a better form of discipline, I used to visualize my old teacher, Master Chung, sitting nearby, watching me with his ever-discerning eye. It helped me avoid drifting off.

When done, I turned and headed for the kitchen shelter. It was the beginning of a beautiful day and I imagined I heard Master Chung laugh and say, "Maybe when you old man like me you have deep breathing inside all time." I smiled.

Mike crawled out of his tent, VHF radio in hand.

"Sounds like a good day . . . sun and the usual strong winds this afternoon. Some mention about a distant front, but no details."

We cooked up a filling breakfast of french toast (lightly covered with maple sugar crystals) and coffee, then leisurely dismantled camp, loaded, and launched into virtually flat waters.

We paddled slowly down the southern side of the Brooks Peninsula and rounded the corner of Jacobson Point. Despite the number of years we'd paddled out here, we'd never gone down to the headwaters of the Nasparti Inlet. Today seemed a good one to do so and to spend the night at the mouth of the Nasparti River, one of the few remaining estuaries not spoiled by the ravages of clearcut logging.

Around the Point we saw a group of kayakers camped in a disgusting spot. The beach was steep and the tents were pitched at a horrendous angle, which must have made for a miserable night's sleep. I surveyed the scene through my binoculars. The sun had yet to strike their cove and everything looked damp. I could see several people pacing the shore, bundled in extra clothing, and I gave forth with a perverse chuckle. Out here, in the bright light of day, we were already hot.

The projected strong winds failed to appear, and with the exception of a gently following swell, the sea lay quiet and calm. From time to time great masses of billowing white clouds drifted over the peaks of the Brooks, blocking out the sun and providing us with a temporary and most welcome coolness. Sometimes a light rain shower would flow down, creating spectacular patterns of light. Faint rainbows would emerge, strengthen in pulsating, vibrant colour, then just as magically dissolve into nothingness.

Eventually we reached the mouth of the Nasparti River and looked about for a site that would be safe from the high waters expected with tonight's tide. We finally chose a spot looking south, down the full length of the inlet, and set to establishing camp. The dense forest rose up steeply behind us, into the peaks of the Refugium Range that ran the length of the Brooks Peninsula.

Later, we paddled our kayaks as far as we could up the Nasparti. When our progress was finally halted by huge jams of uprooted trees, we continued on foot. The pools were deep, and soon we were forced to the river's edge, where we found an exceedingly well-established game trail that wound its way alongside the clear waters.

Eventually we moved out onto a clean gravel bar that sat in the full force of the sun's heat. I stripped and dove into the icy water and emerged screaming, but wonderfully refreshed and clean! The day seemed perfect and gave no hint of what was yet to come.

Back at camp I decided it would be nice to have some fish for dinner, so carried my craft down to the tide line and paddled out, drifting about and casting for the next hour. Very slowly the wind began to strengthen — not in any obvious steady pattern, but with increasing power in the gusts that slid down the mountains. At one point the wind suddenly roared down from both sides of the inlet, the gusts slamming into each other virtually under my kayak. For a moment I was lifted up and suspended in mid-air, then I dropped into the confused waters. It was scary, and I felt it an obvious signal to return to terra firma! I dug my paddle into the water and headed for camp. As I approached, I saw Mike standing at the water's edge, waving me in with strong shoreward gestures. "Deep breathing" started to vanish and "worry mode" kicked into gear. "What's wrong?" I wondered.

When my bow slid onto shore, Mike stood there with VHF radio in hand.

"Not good," he said. "That major system is fast approaching, with storm-force winds from the southeast forecast."

"Storm force" meant wind speeds something in the realm of fifty to fifty-five knots — and on the Brooks the winds always blew stronger. "Southeast" meant the wind would have the full length of the open ocean to gather speed, then be further intensified by the funnel shape of narrow Nasparti Inlet. Our campsite would be the target at the end of all this power. It would also mean that the two-foot safety margin we'd calculated for the high tide would quite probably be obliterated. I continued to sit in my kayak, attempting to absorb the implications of all this new information.

"When's it supposed to hit?" I asked.

"Sometime tomorrow," Mike replied.

I crawled out. I was beat. The thought of dismantling camp, loading, and then having to paddle more than two hours to a protected campsite was not what I wished to contemplate at this point.

"Maybe we should gamble, stay, and just make a really early start in the morning," I suggested.

Just then strange, clunking sounds intruded into our conversation. I turned in the direction they appeared to be coming from, about fifty yards upriver from our tents. One of the largest black bears I'd ever seen was quite casually sauntering the tide line, turning over large rocks with the ease of a giant flicking a pebble aside. The dull clunking was the sound of the falling boulders.

I have a healthy respect for bears. I adhere to the common sense view that this is their turf and I am the intruder. To date, the only problems I'd experienced with bears had been in conventional campgrounds where idiotic people left their garbage about and treated these creatures like harmless fuzzy wuzzys out of a Walt Disney movie. Not to say I hadn't experienced the odd anxious moment when I'd spied a bear coming directly towards me. Still, tension only really increased when I felt I'd trespassed into the bear's "personal" backyard. This seemed to be one of those moments.

"I bet we're right on his route," muttered Mike.

Storm-force winds from the southeast, a large black bear, and the sun close to setting behind the steep peaks.

"What would you do if you were here by yourself?" I asked.

"I'd pack and move," he replied without hesitation.

"If we pack with the speed of magicians, we still won't be off until something like 7:30, and it will take us a good two hours or more to reach our destination. It'll be dark. And the wind seems to be picking up," I moaned.

"Clunk." We both turned. The bear was now closer, well aware of our presence and not the slightest bit perturbed.

"I don't like big bears that seem comfortable with the presence of humans," said Mike. I agreed.

"Besides," I muttered sarcastically, "there's a full moon tonight and I've always wanted to paddle the Brooks under one."

We started loading with astonishing speed. The sound of nearing "clunks" motivated us in a most impressive fashion. Still, it was an arduous chore. Tents and kitchen were dismantled, gear packed in our large bags, then hauled over the estuary mouth to the edge of the distant low tide; then back for the kayaks and more bags of gear. And so it went.

The bear skirted our campsite, then paused and looked my way. I stood by the kayaks, while Mike walked towards me. Then the bear ambled onto the beach between us. It was a tense moment, my back to the ocean and a large bear in front of me. Bruin continued his ritual of lifting giant rocks, eating the morsels underneath, then moving on to the next dinner plate. Eventually he angled off towards the forest. We resumed our task at double time. Then the bear turned and slowly walked in our direction. The last of our gear quickly disappeared into Mike's hatch and in a flash we were in our craft and moving down the inlet.

Already the sun had set, although the day's light still lay softly on the waters well ahead of us. The impending darkness, coupled with an obvious strengthening of wind and sea, produced a healthy level of anxiety. I found the proverbial "second wind" alive and well within me, and it translated into a strong and steady paddling rhythm. To my surprise I found myself ahead of Mike. It was amazing what a little dose of fear could do.

~~~~~~

The Nasparti River soon dissolved into the evening darkness; the bear was now simply a part of the collage of grey and black shapes. The wind increased and we quartered into a building sea flecked with whitecaps. The loss of the sun, coupled with the increasingly rough waters, required constant vigilance on both our parts.

Then we passed out of the darkness into a surreal light. I turned to see a flaming red sun suspended in the valley between two high peaks. We had paddled down the inlet far enough for the sun to appear a second time that day. For a short while we were bathed in its blessed light, then it sank.

"The day of two sunsets," I said to Mike.

"It really is pretty," he said softly, resting his paddle on the cockpit and gazing skyward.

And it was. The mouth of the Nasparti River now lay in a deep blackness; above us, the sky was blanketed in the dying glow of the sun's fire. In the opposite direction the full moon sat well above the horizon and shone down with its late-August intensity. The whitecaps flashed a mixture of brilliant silver and blood-red.

Then out of the deepening night came one last element of wonder.

"Over there," Mike said quietly. "To your right. Killer

whales! Probably the same ones we saw a few days ago."

And there they were, less than a hundred yards away, coming towards us, on a course that would pass us just astern. They looked incredible. Four smooth black bodies broke the stormy surface, dorsal fins cutting the water like sharp-edged knives. They disappeared, then rose again, closer. The increasing wind blew towards them and removed any chance of their sound reaching us. Instead, they moved slowly by, impeccable silent hunters.

We paused and watched. One last time I saw the pod rise. Then they were lost to view in the rough seas and darkening night.

We turned for the shelter of a small cove that lay tucked in an islet, now only fifteen minutes distant. Threatening clouds held back and we paddled to safety on the moon's silver path.